By Susan Laine

Novels
Genie's Wish
Sounds of Love

Novellas
Twice by Chance
The Wolfing Way

Published by Dreamspinner Press
http://www.dreamspinnerpress.com

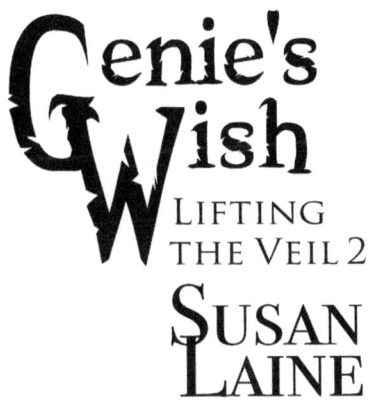

Genie's Wish

LIFTING
THE VEIL 2

SUSAN
LAINE

Dreamspinner Press

Published by
Dreamspinner Press
5032 Capital Circle SW
Ste 2, PMB# 279
Tallahassee, FL 32305-7886
USA
http://www.dreamspinnerpress.com/

Genie's Wish

Cover Art by Shobana Appavu
bob@bob-artist.com

ISBN: 978-1-61372-673-0

Printed in the United States of America
First Edition
August 2012

eBook edition available
eBook ISBN: 978-1-61372-674-7

I would like to dedicate this book to all my readers and to all fans of both the gay romance and paranormal genres alike. Thank you, and enjoy.

Chapter One

"RUB it, Pip, and see what pops up," Valdemar said to Philip, grinning and winking salaciously.

If only it had been a sexual tease, Philip thought ruefully, but alas, it wasn't.

Shoving the ancient electric-blue-and-gold-trimmed oil lamp against Philip's stomach, Valdemar laughed good-naturedly and trotted off like an Arabian stallion. Val Velde might not have been an Arabian, but he was definitely a stud with his stunning blond Viking appearance, sexy sky-blue eyes that could've melted the sun into a pool of jelly, and a bright suggestive smile with pearly white teeth, like some exotic carnivore about to ingest its lunch with a single bite.

Philip had hoped for nearly a year Valdemar would do just that with him—but he never had.

Sighing despondently, Philip turned his attention back to the ancient lamp they'd recovered just today at the archeological dig site at Majlis al-Jinn, the ninth-largest cave chamber in the world—one that after the Great Unveiling had been revealed as a site of an ancient ruined city of unknown origin. The domed cavern of fossiliferous carbonate rock consisted of a single massive chamber 310 meters by 225 meters—and the floor area more than quadrupled after the discovery of the city. Before the Unveiling, the site used to be a favorite hangout of spelunkers, base jumpers, and cave climbers. There were three vertical access points on the freestanding cavern roof, but only one was used.

There was a single entryway into the ruined city from the lowest point of the cave, where two substantial pylons and an arch above a gateway opened up to gigantic stairs leading down into the city proper. Illumination to the city had been provided by the light shafts and their reflections on the light-colored sediment and rock as well as bronze cups of oil that had been lit during the heyday of the palatial city. Remnants of the sweet scented oil had been recovered from these vessels.

Much of the city had been excavated and cleared by flooding and cave-ins, but mostly the city, with its plazas, colonnades, and structures great and small, had been undamaged despite all the time that had passed. Carbon dating of the artifacts found on-site had determined them to be between twelve and fifteen thousand years old, far surpassing even ancient Egyptian culture. The arid desert air kept the structures untouched by the elements, and in the cave the temperature was always a balmy seventeen to eighteen degrees Celsius.

The cavern and the excavated city had been closed to tourists for years now, as it had been classified as a UNESCO Unveiled Heritage Site. Naturally, as the Veil lifting had exposed the well-preserved city virtually intact in this desolate, unpopulated region of the Sultanate of Oman for all the world to see, archaeologists, anthropologists, mythologists, and scientists of a variety of disciplines as well as amateurs, curiosity seekers, and plain old tourists had all flocked to the site.

Ten years later, the site's magnetic pull had diminished considerably, since the rest of the world offered far more exciting—and inhabited—locations for study into the mythical Unseen world.

Still, there was an expedition staying at the site, and Philip Butler was one of the members of this international team of scientists.

Philip, or Pip, as he was called to his infinite dismay, was an archaeologist whose main influence for his choice of career had unfortunately been more Indiana Jones than Kathleen Kenyon or Sir Arthur Evans. Reality had been startlingly different than the glory movies had portrayed, but as he'd learned more and more about archaeology, mythology, and cultures, Philip had found he quite enjoyed digging around in the dirt looking for pieces of pottery in an ancient trash heap, or excavating bones from a burial site, or uncovering any proof of civilization at all.

In three days, their expedition would have been in Majlis al-Jinn for a full year, and less than coincidentally, it was time for their funding to be either renewed—or discontinued. This ancient nameless city of the formerly Unseen world had been a sight for sore eyes in its heyday, but now it lay in ruins, and even though during the first two years after the Great Unveiling there had been back-to-back discoveries made every day, nowadays they actually had to dig around to find anything of interest that would keep the money flowing in.

Having graduated from both Harvard in the US and Oxford in England and now working for the Harvard Semitic Museum, Philip Butler was doing well with his professional career. Sometimes, though, he felt like there was something missing in his life.

And Valdemar Velde, a successful academic and author from Norway by way of Great Britain, an Oxford graduate with three doctorates, gave Philip's heart palpitations to the point of imminent heart failure. Philip couldn't deny his intense instinctive attraction for the Viking god of a man, but to Philip's utter disappointment, Valdemar showed zero interest in him, yet always treated him kindly. Like a friend.

But Philip wanted to get naked with his friend. Maybe he could coax the man into a friendship-with-benefits type of deal?

Going over the possibilities in his vivid imagination like a porno flick, Philip's gaze lowered to the beautiful antique bronze oil lamp, painted electric blue with gold inlay. Even without inspecting the object more closely, Philip could tell it was much younger than the ruined city where it had been found. The age of the city had been estimated at around fifteen to sixteen thousand years.

Digging out a clean handkerchief from his khaki pants pocket, Philip carefully rubbed off the most obvious pieces of dirt and mud stuck on its engraved surface, and even grazed it a bit with his fingertips, relishing the luxury of holding in his hands a concrete piece of history—and mythical history to boot.

A whoosh of air knocked him backward so fast, so far, and so hard that his thick mess of blond hair landed in front of his hazel-brown eyes. Landing on the sandy ground on his ass with a heavy thud, Philip's lungs emptied of precious air, and he had to gasp several times to regain his breath, but he finally managed to push himself up on his elbows.

A bright flash suddenly blinded him, and he had to cover his eyes from the burning hot stream of white light pulsating and roaring like a forest fire.

His senses on overload, Philip wanted to cover his eyes and ears, but with only two hands he failed, and the pain behind his eyelids, in his eardrums, and in his heaving chest increased, like pressure building inside a cooker.

Until....

Shadowy silence washed over him soothingly, and his inner relief mixed with it. Allowing himself to fall on his back on the sand-covered ground, Philip fought for calm and composure now that his senses had reclaimed their serenity.

Carefully sitting up, Philip brushed the thicket that was his unruly hair from his sleepy eyes—and then wished he hadn't.

The man standing in front of him was stark naked.

Oh—my—fucking—God....

All Philip could do was stare, wide-eyed, with his mouth hanging open in surprise.

The man was remarkably tall, maybe six nine or seven feet. If it were possible for a mountain to be reincarnated in male form, this colossal man would've fit the bill to a tee. He had dark tanned skin so silky smooth and hairless, that if it weren't for the iron-black hair cascading down his back, Philip might've thought he'd been born without a hair on him. The man had a muscular athletic frame to die for, and Philip's mouth went as dry as the desert around them as his eyes roamed the vast expanses of broad shoulders, taut belly, narrow hips, and strong long legs—and the thick shaft, perpendicular in its half-hardness before Philip. Chiseled masculine features conflicted with the full sensuous lips, half-parted. Closed heavy-lidded eyes opened slowly, and Philip gaped in amazement and adoration at the electric-blue eyes that shone eerily in the shade of the caves, despite the beams of sunlight above reflected on the yellowish stone walls.

"Oh... my... God...."

It being lunchtime, Philip hadn't even noticed until now how quiet it was here down in the cavern until his voice reverberated and echoed all around.

The strange nude man turned his head, only a black leather collar around his neck, and looked at Philip lying on the ground in front of him, braced up only on his elbows. What an embarrassing spectacle he must've made to this curiosity of a man, Philip thought, and he blushed all over.

A distinct lightning-blue glow flashed in the man's eyes as he studied Philip from head to toe, and his long lashes rimmed his eyes like black curtains. "English.... So, I didn't imagine the endless British chitter-chatter throughout the years after all."

Being half-British and half-American, Philip had a remnant of Oxford English in his accent—and this unknown man had it copied to a tee. That struck Philip silent.

"Who might you be?" the man asked, his head tilted so that his long black hair—so black that it absorbed sunlight—fell to his side as far down as his midsection.

In awe, Philip managed to stammer, "Um, Pip...." The man quirked an amused eyebrow, and Philip blushed again, shaking his head to clear his mind of the blood-red haze of arousal. "I mean... Philip Butler. I'm an archaeologist." That statement earned another curious look from the drop-dead gorgeous man, whose lean frame shifted, and hard muscles moved beneath the dark skin like some kind of majestic beasts. "That's the study of human society through evidence of the past, like artifacts, structures, cultural relics...." His voice fading, Philip tried to gain some insight into the man in front of him, at least to discern whether the man was actually listening or interested, but his look remained the same—a curious, amused detachment with warm glowing eyes and curved full lips. "Anyway... I'm here to study this ruin," he added, waving his hand around in a general gesture, indicating the ruined state of affairs of the palatial string of structures at the bottom of the cavern at Majlis al-Jinn, extending far beyond what had once been solid rock.

This time the man's look changed, turning darker and more dangerous for an instant as his inspective gaze traveled the archaeological site before it landed back on Philip. "You can see the city?"

That Philip had not expected. "Yes...."

"You must be *special,* then," the man said, his voice smooth and seductive and his blue eyes striking in their appreciation as they wandered all over Philip's body.

"I, uh...," Philip muttered, fighting for comprehension and clarity but succeeding in neither pursuit, and all the while those shining eyes made their leisurely journey on his figure, giving him goose bumps and arousing his cock into a salute.

As if aware of the reaction he was causing, the man stepped forward—still butt naked—and extended his hand. "Here, allow me to help you get back on your feet—" A sharp clank stopped him, and the oil lamp he must've accidentally kicked jumped and glided on the sandy ground, landing in front of Philip's feet. Leaning down to grasp the lamp, the man's fingers brushed only air when the lamp moved away from his touch as if it had a mind of its own, bouncing into Philip's lap.

"Oh... my... God...," Philip mumbled, hugging the ancient oil lamp close to his chest and staring at the peculiar man all wide-eyed, like a surprised child watching Santa actually climb down a chimney.

The unusual man grinned. "Sadly, no. But I'm flattered."

Philip frowned. "No, I mean...." The man's grin widened, like the Cheshire cat, and as his cheeks flushed red, Philip stumbled to his feet, clutching the lamp tightly. "You... you're a... a genie.... A lamp genie...."

"The proper term, I believe, is a jinn," the man corrected, his sensuous lips curving into a sweet smile that made Philip's knees buckle. "But in general, yes, that would be a fair and accurate assessment."

While Philip was busy ogling the mythical apparition before him, standing there so very much in the flesh, he suddenly heard faint voices approaching from the distance. Someone was coming down toward the main palace from either the staircase or the elevator that had both been added to the site soon after the Great Unveiling, when it turned out that at the bottom of the site stood a palatial city stretching deep into what had formerly been solid rock.

"Oh my God...," he mumbled in abject horror, staring in the direction lost in the shade of the palatial structures now lying in ruins.

"You do say that a lot," the man noted from his side. "Any particular deity you're trying to invoke or commune with?"

"Wha—" Philip's fixed look held those electric-blue eyes that he was now close enough to see were filled with tiny lightning bursts of powers beyond his imagination. He had to shake his head to clear his vision and his mind of this bizarre man. "No. Don't talk."

"I do not take kindly to commands that aren't presented as wishes." A warning loomed beneath the surface, like a shark prowling the shallow waters of Philip's pond.

"Wha—" In passing Philip realized he sounded like a broken record, and he blushed deeply. "No. That's not what I meant." The sounds of footsteps and voices came closer, and Philip froze. "Please, don't speak. Let me handle this. Please...?" Philip's hazel eyes pleaded with the... genie... for understanding.

Suddenly the man relaxed again and grinned with a wink. "As you wish... Pip."

Blushing for the umpteenth time, Philip suddenly remembered that the man—the genie—was still completely nude. "Oh my God...," he mumbled as his eyes traveled in shock and awe across the masculine apparition before him, and that action earned him an amused chuckle in response. Philip began to believe that spontaneous human combustion would be a preferable option to all this intense blushing.

Waving someone off, Valdemar appeared on the scene, with his usual laid-back grin and suggestive eyes. Philip thought that he'd seriously suffer a nervous breakdown when he came face to face with a naked lamp genie.

And sure enough, Valdemar's sky-blue eyes lit up like a bonfire upon seeing Philip's mysterious visitor. Even through the irrational and hopeless surge of jealousy and envy that coursed through his veins, Philip longed to speak, to try to explain the situation somehow—though he had no idea how, exactly. He ended up opening his mouth but saying nothing and finally closing it before flies swarmed in—not that there were any in the desert.

"Who might you be?" Valdemar asked, still smiling, and, scared out of his mind, Philip turned to look at the genie—who *was* wearing clothes.... They were similar to Philip's own: simple brown khaki pants, white button-down shirt, and brown mountaineering boots. On the genie, however, the clothes didn't hang unflatteringly as they did on Philip, who was slim to the point of thin and bony, but instead they fit him like a glove, showcasing that perfect masculine physique like a smooth second skin. As far as the colors were concerned, in essence, Philip—like the genie—would've been able to camouflage himself like a chameleon in his desert surroundings, if he so chose. Sometimes Philip felt invisible no matter what he was wearing.

Like right now, when the guy he'd lusted after for a year was lusting after *his* genie.

Now that was a strange thought, Philip considered in passing, and he glanced at the genie. Upon finding the genie smiling at him almost lewdly, he blushed.

"I'm a friend of Pip's," the genie replied smoothly.

"Pip, huh?" Valdemar said, his gaze shifting to Philip, who almost stated a wish for the earth to open up and swallow him whole.

But he didn't get his wish. What he got instead.... "A close, personal friend," the genie clarified, winking at Philip in a way that left little doubt in anyone's mind about what he was referring to. The flash of heat that flooded Philip's groin brought his cock into painful contact with the confines of his zipper, and he had to shift his stance to readjust and relieve the pressure.

Philip shot a glance from the genie's electric-blue eyes to Valdemar's sky-blue eyes. What an odd triangle they made, Philip pondered, as he stared at Valdemar, who stared at the genie, who stared at Philip, who stared at....

Suddenly the genie said something, but Philip couldn't understand a word. But Valdemar's eyes grew wide, and he grinned happily. Realizing that the genie had spoken in Norwegian only increased Philip's disappointment at again being left out of the equation. Valdemar laughed and playfully slapped the genie's muscular arm, holding the touch just long enough for it not to be accidental but almost a sensual message. While the two of them kept talking, Philip felt as he always did with Val—unimportant, unattractive, disappointed, and jealous.

"It's so wonderful to be able to converse in my native tongue," Valdemar finally said, glancing at Philip from under his long blond lashes and including him in the conversation—but as far as Philip was concerned, it was a little too late. As usual, he was the third wheel. "So, lunch anyone?" Valdemar added with exaggerated enthusiasm, his gaze moving between the two men as he clapped his hands together.

Philip refused with a curt shake of his head, and the genie said only, "Alas, I must regretfully decline. My appetites require adherence to strict dietary requirements."

"Another time, then," Valdemar replied courteously, bowing his head slightly in a very gentlemanly manner that Philip found charming—and irritating. Turning to Philip, Valdemar raised his eyebrows. "Did you catalog that lamp yet, Pip?" He nodded at the oil lamp Philip was still holding against his chest—and instinctively Philip clutched it tighter, as if Valdemar were attempting to snatch it from him then and there.

"I'll add it to the site inventory soon, but I'm going to check out the exact recovery location first," Philip said, hoping his tone was as level as he was attempting to keep it.

Valdemar's eyes flashed, and he opened his mouth as if to ask something but then just shrugged, as if thinking better of it. "All right, then. Don't forget, though," he reminded him. Then he flashed an amazing smile at the genie and walked away toward the elevator.

Philip let out a long sigh, as if he'd been holding his breath the entire time, but even that wasn't enough to completely relax him. He suspected that only magically turning back time to the point when the oil lamp was discovered—and then not finding the damn thing—would do the trick and put him at ease.

But as it was, the sexy genie in front of him was all too real to pretend otherwise.

"Is he to be your first wish, then?" the genie asked all of a sudden, startling Philip out of his reverie. "I can see that you desire him."

"Wha—" Philip was dumbfounded. "Wish...?" And then the reality of the situation finally dawned on him. He had a genie at his beck and call, and he could wish for anything—even for Valdemar Velde in his bed. The possibility of that dream coming true shook him to the core, which surprised him since he'd never thought of himself as the possessive type. "Oh God... I need a chair or something...," he mumbled, feeling his legs shaking and knees buckling.

The genie chuckled low. "Is a chair to be your first wish, Pip?"

That husky, seductive amusement was like a bucket of ice-cold water on his back, and it was exactly what he needed to cool down. "Ha ha, very funny." Checking the genie out as calmly as he could, he asked, "What's your name? What can I call you?"

The genie grinned teasingly. "Anything you wish, Pip."

"Funny guy," Philip said, exasperated, but then he took a breath to mellow himself out again. "Please?"

The full, kissable lips of the genie curved into a curious smile. "You're a queer little mortal, aren't you?" *Oh, you have no idea.* "I am no longer allowed to use my true name, so you can call me Jinn."

"Why aren't you allowed to say your own name?"

"Why do you think, Pip?"

"Does it have anything to do with why you were trapped inside the lamp?"

"Very good," Jinn complimented Philip with a lascivious grin. "My name was added to the list of the accursed ones, same as the others. A punishment for my wicked ways of life."

Philip frowned. "What did you do?"

"That, I think, is a discussion best shared at another time," Jinn said vaguely.

"Um, okay…," Philip stated, unsure of himself. He'd become an archaeologist because he fared better with things long dead and gone than with people in the here and now. "How can you speak English, or Norwegian, for that matter?"

Jinn chuckled in response. "I am a genie. With your friend Val, I could sense his unspoken dreams. As a wish-granting genie, I'm privy to the deepest desires and hushed wishes of the mortal breed." Jinn winked at him. "Just like I can sense your hopes and dreams, Pip. How you want Val, for instance."

Philip blushed and bit his lip angrily. "That's private. And none of your business."

Jinn shrugged, but then his eyes flashed intently. "Your friend—"

"Colleague," Philip corrected, since Valdemar was nothing personal to him at all.

"He could see this place as well. One person—a coincidence. Two—not so much. Has something... happened?"

Letting out a deep breath, Philip nodded carefully. "The Great Unveiling. Ten years ago, the Veil between the Unseen world and the mundane world was lifted. We still don't know why, and we may never know." Sighing ruefully and plopping down on the ground on his ass, Philip said quietly, "So... I'm not special."

Jinn kneeled in front of him with a curiously tender smile tugging a corner of his lips. "I disagree with that assessment—but that's beside the point. The whole world knows, then? Well, that's something new to get used to...."

"A wish...," Philip muttered under his breath, inspecting the genie in front him, Jinn's long black hair brushing against his hands on his bent knees. "So, you really *are* a genie...."

"Indeed I am, dear boy," Jinn replied, chuckling. Apparently he found Philip too amusing to be regarded as anything else.

"So...." Philip pensively followed the train of thought to its conclusion, tilting the lamp in his hands. "Even though you're standing—or kneeling—in front of me, you're actually trapped in this oil lamp. Hell, you can't even touch it." He looked up into the genie's eyes, which sparkled like lightning showers, mystified by the way the day had turned out—but still himself, regardless of how many miracles a day held. "Can I wish for your freedom?"

Those piercing blue eyes glimmered dangerously. "You would waste a perfectly good wish on poor little old me, would you, Pip?" Jinn's neutral tone remained undecipherable, but for some reason the lowness of it gave Philip goose bumps.

Frowning and puckering his lips, Pip shook his head, infuriated. "I don't consider it a waste. But yes, I would. So, can I?"

Suddenly Jinn chuckled contentedly. "Your reply speaks to a high degree of personality and a kind, giving soul. You honor me,

Pip." Jinn bowed his head slowly, placing his hand over his heart, before he continued coolly, "You're sweet, to be sure, Pip. But alas, it is not necessary on your part to make such a sacrifice on my behalf, I assure you." Jinn offered his hand to Philip, who took it gratefully and got up again. "So, what is your first wish to be, master?"

Philip shook his head emphatically, chagrined. "Please don't call me that."

Jinn chuckled. "As you wish."

Actually feeling the blood drain from his paling face, Philip stammered, "No, no, that wasn't a—"

"A mere joke, Pip," Jinn interjected, winking—and giving Philip a rush of feeling somewhere between annoyance and arousal.

"With that flippant tongue of yours, I'm not surprised in the least that you got yourself imprisoned in that lamp," Philip huffed, exasperated. But upon seeing Jinn's sensuous smile the emotion vanished, and all he felt was a kind of mellow satisfaction. Then worry washed over him, and he looked down at the lamp he was still holding. "What do I do with the lamp?"

Jinn's fiery gaze landed on the lamp as well, and the curve of his voluptuous lips drew serious. "Keep it hidden until you've made all three wishes."

Fear made Philip panic, and he knew that he sounded like a scared kid, but even though he could die or kill for someone he loved, in essence Philip was a devout pacifist. As such, fear always seemed to be his first reaction—and it annoyed him to no end. "You mean someone could—"

Jinn's expression was grave. "Yes. You must safeguard the lamp from anyone who might seek to take it—and me—from you." Quickly, however, his face relaxed and reacquired that sultry look that turned Philip's knees all rubbery. "If all goes well, you will be my last master, Pip. With that in mind, please, ask for something wild and imaginative."

"What do you mean by… last master?" Philip asked, curious.

"The Unveiling. Jinns are powerful beings, and mortals can only have a hold over us as long as the world remains unaware of our true nature. As it stands, the world now knows about my kind. Enslaving me will not be easy for any mortal ever again, as the rules binding our demure, slavish conduct are long since passed, what with the Unveiling and all."

"Oh, I see," Philip said with obvious relief. "That's what you meant when you told me I don't need to wish for your freedom." Jinn merely bowed his head in acknowledgement of Philip's realization. A sudden burst of exciting possibilities overcame Philip's fear and weakness and caused his face to flush with heat. "Can you really do… anything… I wish?"

Stepping closer until their chests were all but touching, Jinn grinned. "Anything your little mortal heart desires, Pip. We the Jinn are very powerful beings. We can change the world with a snap of our fingers, travel through time, give a breath of life to each and every one of your fantasies. In a word, yes, anything. But bear in mind you only have *three* wishes. No wishing for a hundred more, understand? That kind of silly stunt would only irk me."

Knowing in his heart he needed time to reflect on all that he'd heard, Philip also knew that keeping the lamp hidden would be next to impossible. Above ground, the expedition site was composed of no more than nine tents, and had zero security other than the poorly constructed aluminum fence that anyone could climb over and the weekly patrol of less-than-efficient local law enforcement. It was in no way sufficient to protect the lamp—if he told anyone about it in the first place. And if he didn't, he'd have to hide it among his belongings—in open tents with no locks, and if someone did find it, he'd be charged with attempted larceny, and his career would be over and done with.

Biting his lower lip nervously, Philip realized he had only two options. One, to confide in someone he trusted—and despite his strong amorous feelings toward Valdemar, he wasn't sure if the man was trustworthy, as he was a consummate professional and ethically honorable to a fault. And that wasn't much of a choice anyway, because even if Valdemar was willing to help, Philip would be putting his career, and maybe his life too, in danger—and that was unacceptable.

Sighing, he looked up at Jinn, resigned. "Can you make the lamp small enough so I can hide it on my person, for example like a... a toy dangling on a key chain, or something?"

Those full, sensual lips curved into a curious smile, as if the genie were trying to decipher the riddle that was Philip—only he felt too boring and uninteresting to be considered any kind of mystery. He was the complete opposite of Valdemar, who had it all—good looks, charismatic presence, magnetic sex appeal, witty charm, sophisticated manners, smart and funny personality.... Philip was depressing himself more by the minute. Jinn's reply tore him out of his glum reverie. "I can do anything you wish, Pip. I told you that."

Slowly, Philip nodded. "But... only as long as it's presented as a wish, right?"

Jinn bowed his head slightly. "Exactly right, master. I can only use my powers freely when I am finally free. No sooner. As long as I'm tied to the lamp, my powers are limited to wishes requested." The mesmerizing eyes of the genie in front of Philip shifted between his gaze and the magical lamp he was holding against his fast-beating heart.

Exhaling slowly, Philip nodded in acceptance of his decision. "I suppose wording is the key here, huh? Never mind. Don't answer. All right, then, here we go." Taking several deep breaths, as if preparing for a physical exertion, Philip said firmly, "I wish for you to reduce this magical oil lamp of yours to a more manageable size so that I can fit it on this—" Philip dug out his key chain from his pocket. "—on this key chain."

A bright flash shot out from those piercing blue eyes, like lightning striking, but even blinded, Philip distinctly heard the snap of Jinn's powerful fingers. "Your wish is my command."

Blinking to regain his temporarily lost sight, Philip felt more than saw the magic lamp shrinking in his hands until he could detect only a cute little toy resting on his right palm. Quickly, he set out to attach the toylike magic lamp onto his key chain by the lamp's handle, scanning around in a manner that could only be described as utterly paranoid. Yet he worried someone had seen him—and would soon come to tear Jinn away from him and end the world with power-hungry selfish wishes. Yes, for Philip the glass was mostly half-empty, and he always expected the worst-case scenario to come to pass. It wasn't the healthiest view of life—he knew that—and he did believe he'd have an ulcer the size of the Grand Canyon by the time he was thirty-five.

Sighing in relief as he stuck the key chain back into the dark, warm safety of his pocket, Philip dared a half smile. "Well, that's done."

"Yes." Jinn smiled back—only his gesture was predatory. "One down, two to go."

Now why did that ominous statement sound like the infamous last words? Philip wondered, concerned. It took considerable effort on his part to push the trepidation out of his mind and get his meager figure moving toward the elevator at the star-shaped Khoshilat Beya Al Hiyool entrance, also known as the Asterisk, and the expedition encampment awaiting topside. Hiding the genie would prove to be a challenge for anyone, but Philip swore to himself to keep Jinn safe. No one would take advantage of him.

Not even Philip himself.

Chapter Two

"WHO are we so cautious about?" Jinn asked in a hushed tone, following in Philip's footsteps.

"Shh!" Philip cut in with a loud whisper, looking like a child pretending to be a spy and not having a clue as to how to be inconspicuous.

Arriving at Philip's tent without drawing unwanted attention to themselves proved difficult for Philip, who kept glancing around furtively, and that, more than anything, could've caught everyone's notice. Fortunately, the encampment was virtually deserted, as the members of the expedition—both the academicians and the hired muscle—were packed tight in the tent serving as the common dining area. Jinn watched with a mix of amusement and irritation at Philip's surreptitious skulking until he snuck stealthily into his own tent with a guilty look on his face, as if he were trespassing on his own private grounds.

"Are you all right, Jinn?" Philip asked immediately, anxious, rushing to close the tent flaps and skittishly glancing all around outside before finally doing it.

"You are such a queer little mortal, Pip." Jinn chuckled. Genies were immortal, with godlike powers, so, unafraid of whatever might happen if he wasn't paying attention, he stoically held his ground against the frantic behavior of Philip as the archaeologist ran around securing the tent as if he expected someone to try and slip in under his nose and steal what amounted to a common-looking oil lamp toy on a key chain.

Pausing at Jinn's remark, Philip then staggered nervously and blushed all over. This young mortal certainly was a quaint little thing, Jinn noted, and he observed Philip sitting down on his travel bed heavily, as if the weight of the world hung on his slim shoulders.

In Jinn's experience, all manner of men could function in society, but it was a rare breed of men who forcefully cut their way through all obstacles and claimed their place as conquerors, victors, and rulers. Philip matched none of those images of ideal manhood. Short in stature, slender in figure, and shy in his behavior, Philip left much to be desired in terms of masculine prowess—and yet Jinn found himself unable to look away from this new kind of man. Not feminine, exactly, but far from the bulky, beefy warrior types and the rigid, standoffish ruler types.

To his surprise, Jinn found he quite liked Philip's version of manhood.

But a more immediate concern for Jinn was the fact that these fabrics he wore made him itch and sweat in a most unpleasant way. He had to get out of them or risk suffocation. Besides… he preferred his own attire to this strange clothing covering up what was one of his finest features—his body.

Philip was busy hanging his head, distressed or depressed or something, as far as Jinn could tell. He heard the man mumbling incoherently but figured it wasn't intended for his ears, so he focused on snapping his fingers and changing his attire.

Staring down at himself after the alteration, Jinn smiled happily. "Ah, that's much better."

From the bed Philip looked up—and then sprang to his feet as if the bed had been on fire. And his horrified look was positively hilarious, in Jinn's humble opinion. "Oh my God…. You can't dress like *that*. Are you mad? No one wears anything like that today—unless it's a masquerade ball or a costume party. You have to change. Right now."

"What is wrong with what I wear?" Jinn wondered out loud, bemused. "This is the latest in fashion." Spreading his arms by his sides, he took a good long look at the shiny blue silk pants that looked like flowing robes in their looseness, the open blue silk vest—and nothing else.

Philip looked shocked. "Where? The Playboy Mansion?"

That reference meant nothing to Jinn, who calmly inquired, "Do tell me, Pip, what it is in your opinion that I should be wearing." To emphasize his point of acquiescing to any and all of Philip's demands, Jinn snapped his fingers—and was immediately disrobed into full nudity as his new magical clothes vanished into thin air, revealing the sun-kissed skin with strong muscles rippling under it. Jinn was becoming more and more entranced by Philip's lovely, innocent eyes staring at him.

"Oh my God…," Philip said loudly, first unable to veer his gaze away from the sight Jinn knew well was as tempting and lusty as a naked masculine man could possibly be, but then he lifted his hands as fast as a lightning bolt to block his eyes. "Cover yourself…." And he kept repeating those same two words rapidly, as if they were the only two words left in the English language.

Chuckling at the endearing sight of sexy insecurity, Jinn walked quietly up to Philip, stopping right in front of him. The young man's natural, slightly musky scent pervaded his olfactory senses, with hints of tea, honey, dust, and sand giving off their own unique whiffs. Still continuing his mindless, unintelligible chatter, Philip remained unaware of Jinn's proximity—and that only intensified the experience for Jinn.

Sexually, Jinn had always been omnivorous, finding pleasure and delight wherever it was offered or could be taken. The chase had its rewards, and Jinn found himself irrevocably excited at the nearness of this nearly rail-thin young man who shivered at the mere image of Jinn nude in his imagination. There was something special about Pip that called out to Jinn, and Jinn had been stuck in that cursed lamp for far too long.

Sparks of arousal kindled beneath his skin, enflaming his groin, and his cock reacted feverishly, swelling and rising swiftly and easily to rock hardness and fire hotness. Philip was shorter than Jinn by a good two heads' height, and desirously he studied the sandy-blond hair, straight strands with slight curls around the temples, ears, and neck. Philip's hair smelled like fresh apples and desert wind and looked so silky soft that Jinn lifted his right hand to find out for himself if that was truly the case.

Jinn's fingers brushed the few blond strands behind the young mortal's ear—and Philip's hazel eyes shot wide open in sudden surprise. Gently cupping Philip's cheek with his large palm, Jinn whispered, "Allow me to serve you, master."

Stepping back in a rush of angry movement, Philip's face stiffened in outrage. "I told you before *not* to call me that. And let me be absolutely crystal clear here: you are *not* my sex slave or servant of any kind."

Philip's youthful innocence and instinctive selflessness turned Jinn on to no end, and he barely held himself in check. Yes, he could've used his considerable powers to secure Pip's love and compliance without him realizing it, and it would not have been the first time he'd used his masculine sex appeal to win over a wish master's heart. With Philip, however, Jinn had an inexplicable urge to seduce the man the natural way rather than use his magical wiles to get him to succumb.

"I apologize for causing you discomfort, Pip. I only wanted to touch you."

Disbelief, suspicion, and nervousness all flickered in Philip's wary eyes. "Why?"

At that Jinn had to laugh, and he wondered in passing if he was able to hide his own bewilderment from this perceptive guy. "I do hope you're not serious, Pip." He raked his gaze all over Philip's slender, supple figure. "I desire you."

Philip's eyes widened to the point of almost popping right out of his head. Sliding his hand slowly down to caress Philip's tender jawline, where there wasn't even a trace of stubble, Jinn thumbed the young man's lusciously full lower lip. Philip started to shake and blink fiercely. "P-please, d-don't play games with me, Jinn…." The trembling of his tone was a clear indication to Jinn that he might have crossed the line of how much the young man was comfortable with. And yet, he could smell Philip's arousal, and knew that his quarry required only a wee nudge to give in to what his body craved.

And from Jinn's point of view, it wouldn't hurt Philip's chances at pursuing the man he did consciously want—Val—if that man believed he was going to miss out on Philip altogether.

"I am not toying with you, Pip," he assured him softly, sweetly. "Surely you are aware that I have coveted you from the first moment our eyes met?"

Unable and unwilling to control his appetite any longer, Jinn lifted Philip's chin carefully, giving the man ample opportunity to pull back if he really didn't want this, and then leaned down, brushing a ghost of kiss over the lips that held such power of life within them. Mortals were rarely conscious of their true significance in the grand scheme of things, in the fervent dance of life between the thresholds of birth and death. As a genie, Jinn knew these liminal states all too well.

With one kiss Jinn stole Philip's breath—and all vestiges of his resistance. This Jinn construed from the rapid heartbeat, full-body shivers, and buckling knees Philip was sporting. And then those slim arms wrapped around his shoulders for support as that lithe body leaned against him, and Jinn tilted his head to the side to deepen the kiss, swiping the tip of his tongue along the seam of Philip's quivering lips until they parted and allowed Jinn entry.

Delectable and fragrant was the taste and smell of Philip's mouth that Jinn relished from the first lick as the flavors reached his senses, and he felt that flash of heat from head to toes. Mortals had such a short life span that they gave in to their wants with all their heart, body, and soul, and as Jinn curled his tongue around Philip's and sucked it into his own mouth, he could not have been happier at that fact.

With a wanton sigh, Philip had all but succumbed to his inner desires when he suddenly fought against the embrace, and Jinn relinquished his hold ever so slightly until their lips parted and broke the kiss. Obviously seeking any excuse to cut short their passionate assignation, Philip asked breathlessly, "Is this just because you're horny after all those years spent in captivity?"

"No." Jinn shook his head and resumed kissing his sweet wish master.

And again Philip resisted, discontinuing the kiss. "Is this merely because I'm here and convenient for you to—"

"No." This time Jinn heard the impatience in his own voice and knew he was nearing the point of no return when he'd ravage his lovely mortal master and claim him as his lover regardless of any and all objections. Plunging right back into the thick of things, Jinn reclaimed Philip's luscious lips once more.

Aborting the kiss for a third time, Philip wrangled to free himself from Jinn's arms but failed. "Is this—"

Interrupting his reluctant lover with a chuckle, Jinn asked amusedly, "Are you always this suspicious of the ulterior motives of potential lovers when all they desire is to keep kissing you for an interminable amount of time?"

Philip had the good grace to blush all over, causing Jinn's blood to boil with want. "I am skeptical of things that seem too good to be true, yes, and analytical of apparent miracles and—"

"You mean overthinking every little detail," Jinn said, cutting him off, keeping his tone light as he coaxed the young man into a kind of levity, intent on not scaring him off.

Philip shivered and swallowed, but no longer attempted to escape Jinn's clutches as emphatically as he had before. "I'm a scientist and a scholar, a rational and thoughtful professional. I'm not supposed to...." His voice trailed off as he fought to find the right words.

"To what?" Jinn inquired, curious. "To have sex? Now what kind of silly rule is that?"

"Avoiding familiarities and fraternization enhances workplace productivity and—" Philip said, his tone uncertain, stammering slightly, but from his hazel eyes Jinn understood he really and truly believed at least a portion of his own assertions. And yet his body disagreed.

"Rules are meant to be broken."

Jinn's interruption caused Philip to stare at him with a strange expression on his face, part admiration, part dismay. Jinn found that contradiction of intellect and emotion irresistible.

"Yes, well, as a rebellious individual who has already been punished for your fun and games and placed in a cursed oil lamp for all eternity, Jinn, you *would* make that argument," he stated, frowning.

Not quite sure whether Philip was actually angry or just riling him up, Jinn nonetheless felt only abashed amusement over the situation. Cooing at the man with those childlike wide eyes, Jinn murmured appeasingly, "Oh, Pip.... Let's not argue. I'd much rather make up...." Tightening his hold on Philip once more, Jinn brushed his lips tenderly over Philip's soft cheek, tasting the salt of fresh sweat and the musk of his natural flavor, and opened his mouth to lick and suckle on the soft spot beneath his ear for good measure. "Mmm... oh, by the gods you taste divine," he whispered in hungry appreciation.

With his eyes closed, Jinn felt Philip succumb to sensual rapture as his wobbly knees buckled, and weakly Philip pressed his lithe figure against Jinn's bulkier form. Carefully, not wishing to push his lover-to-be to panicky flight, Jinn maneuvered Philip toward the travel bed with its easily assembled, light metallic frame and rather uncomfortable-looking solid mattress. Sliding his hands down his wish master's back, Jinn cupped Philip's butt and scooped him up from the floor into his lap, aligning their swelling, hardening cocks until they rubbed against each other in sensual friction.

Philip moaned low, winding his arms around Jinn's neck in a libidinous act of lust he no longer held in check. This was how Jinn wanted to see Philip—in the throes of sexual ecstasy. Lowering Philip on his back on the makeshift bed, Jinn felt his young lover arch up to gain greater contact, and Jinn obliged by placing his body down over Philip's but bracing himself with his hands to hold off most of his weight.

Jinn's lips traveled passionately from Philip's lips past his clean-shaven cheek to his soft neck, feeling the throbbing vein there and sucking the skin softly for the blood to come surging closer until a hickey formed. "Sweet, Pip. You taste so sweet and scrumptious and delectable." Associations with eating were not lost on Jinn, who craved more.

"Jinn...." Philip's low mumble was a hush of passion, giving Jinn's heart palpitations.

Warm skin and nubile limbs greeted Jinn as his hands wandered and roamed around Philip's clad body. Too many layers of fabric separated them, and Jinn fumbled with the buttons of Philip's khaki pants. Buttons were not Jinn's specialty, but as a genie he was a fast learner, and soon enough the waistband and the fly with their annoying buttons popped open to reveal Philip's cotton underwear.

Philip tightened his hold on Jinn's arms, trembling, and a hint of desperate need colored the reaction. Jinn was apparently right to assume that it had been a while for both of them and that Jinn wasn't the only who needed this. Only... Philip's true desires ran in another direction, and Jinn was beginning to more than need what was about to happen between them. He started to want it. To want Philip—whose heart belonged to another man.

"Do you wish me to stop, Pip?" he asked concernedly, wanting to hear the answer but afraid to hear it also.

Philip's baffled face came up to meet his, and he seemed utterly confused. "Y-you mean I can only have this with you if it's a wish...?"

The earnest disappointment in his tone undid Jinn, who rushed to say, "Of course not, Pip. I only meant to ask you if you are sure you want me to make love to you. Because you... well, you do want someone else... too."

Jinn was beginning to fall in love with Philip's fierce blushing and with that shy curve of a smile twitching at the corner of his lips. A kind of sadness invaded Philip's delicate features, and ruefully he said, "What I feel... he doesn't share. How long should I wait for him to notice me?"

Jinn leaned on his elbow next to Philip's side and slowly caressed his rumpled neckline, playing with the buttons of his shirt, undoing them one by one so slowly that his intention of giving Philip more time to consider his actions could not be misconstrued. "Maybe, Pip, what you need to do is stop waiting for him to spot you—and make him see you."

The fascinating shade of Philip's eyes, that light dusky color of hazel brown, darkened as Philip gazed up at Jinn's own eyes, and Jinn saw astonishment there. Jinn could relate to his bewilderment as he had never missed an opportunity to seduce a new lover—which is what had gotten him into the trouble in the first place.

"Y-you don't want to...?" Insecurity poured off Philip in waves, and Jinn could not for the life of him understand how this lovely young man could not know how attractive and desirable he truly was.

"Oh, Pip, I absolutely want to...," he drawled alluringly, and he proceeded to convince his wish master of the veracity of his statement by pushing his hand underneath Philip's underwear and wrapping his fist around the long, slender cock that was fast filling up with blood and stood up to reach for Jinn's touch. The nest of pubes and the heat were nothing new to Jinn, but the silky smooth shaft was. "You feel... different from other men, Pip...."

His amazed comment caused Philip to chuckle while panting. "Oh, right, I'm cut. I've been circumcised." And there went the cute reddening of cheeks, neck, and chest again. Of the latter Jinn could only detect a sliver through the parted collar of Philip's shirt, turning him on. This new form of the male member that already tickled his sensual fancy was the most arousing thing he'd experienced in ages—and in his case saying that was no exaggeration.

Stroking and pumping the eagerly jerking dick in his hand, Jinn was well aware that, being naked again, he could not hide his own arousal from Philip. And as predicted, Philip's eyes came down, heavy-lidded, to watch not only Jinn's palm working his cock but the heavy, thick cock poking his thigh through the fabric of his pants. The blaze within those pretty eyes set Jinn on fire in equal measure. Jinn welcomed Philip's hungry gaze as it inspected every inch of Jinn's cock, with its imposing girth, mouthwatering dark hue, and spear-like length.

"Y-you're beautiful, Jinn," Philip whispered, and from his hushed tone it was clear to Jinn that Philip made such utterances rarely, if ever. No wonder he had difficulties with making his feelings known to Valdemar Velde, the charismatic adventurer-archaeologist.

Jinn smiled and met Philip in a kiss, slow and lingering, wet and deep and profound. "I am delighted that you think I'm worth seeing, Pip." Laughing gently into the kiss, Philip wound his arms around Jinn's neck, the muscles and tendons there strong as those of an ox, and broad shoulders that could've held up the entire world. Once Jinn had, too—figuratively speaking.

A loud cough came from the tent doorway. "Excuse me...."

Both Jinn and Philip's heads popped up from the bed to find Valdemar standing before the tent flaps he'd discreetly and considerately closed behind him. *Well, Val sure saw Pip now.* Jinn had no delusions about the kind of picture he and Philip made, Philip with his rumpled clothes and arousal scenting his skin, and Jinn with his excited nakedness.

As Philip struggled to scramble to his feet, Jinn moved away more slowly to give Philip the time and opportunity to deny that anything was going on. Knowing Philip's feelings, long held true for Valdemar, Jinn fully expected Philip to do so. Pulling the cotton sheet over to cover his dwindling erection, Jinn waited silently, sitting on the bed and watching Valdemar stand restlessly at the front of the tent, shifting his weight from one foot to another, his sky-blue eyes darting all over the place—anywhere but at Philip or Jinn.

And having experience at seduction, emotions, and sexual heat, Jinn had zero trouble discerning the silent dismay and burning jealousy barely concealed in those blue eyes.

Philip was too busy tucking his shirt back in his pants and buttoning up tight to notice that. From the sidelines, Jinn observed quietly how embarrassed, nervous, and ashamed Philip looked—but saw also the frustration and anger there. Biting his lower lip, Philip said hoarsely, "I realize that here we live in tents and all, Val, but you should've knocked."

Both Jinn and Valdemar stared dumbfounded at Philip, who'd regained his composure and had his steady, slightly scolding gaze fixed on Valdemar—who surprisingly blushed across his porcelain white face, and a swarm of golden freckles emerged as a result.

Licking his dry lips and looking decidedly uncomfortable, Valdemar nodded in agreement. "I offer my sincerest apologizes, Pip—uh, I mean Philip." Adding the name correction clearly reluctantly, Valdemar glanced at the so obviously bare-bottomed Jinn, and the manner with which he gritted his teeth and shot daggers at him with his eyes did not go unnoticed by Jinn. It seemed Philip had made a conquest without realizing it, Jinn pondered. He felt a sudden stab of jealousy mixing with envy, and his own eyes returned the chagrined look right back to Valdemar.

As it turned out, Jinn thought glumly, the reality of this ridiculous situation was that while Philip thought no one could possibly be seriously interested in him, there were now, in fact, not one, but *two* men competing for his affections.

"Is something wrong?" Philip inquired politely.

Valdemar opened his mouth to snap something but, blinking furiously, swallowed his intended words and said, "Mr. Moneyman will be arriving by nightfall." Valdemar and Philip shared an exasperated sigh and an annoyed expression that spoke to Jinn about the commonalities the two shared. "He'll go over the most recent reports and check the findings—and review the books. That's why I came over. Did you finish the cataloguing for the day before you...." Valdemar's voice trailed off, and Philip blushed but lifted his chin in almost an act of defiance, if Jinn interpreted the gesture correctly. Clearing his throat awkwardly, Valdemar finished by saying, "I was thinking of the oil lamp, of course."

"Of course, Val. I never expected anything else," Philip replied coolly, but Jinn heard his disappointment. The following lie that rolled off his tongue so elegantly did, however, surprise Jinn. "I took the lamp to the appraisal tent, but I'll finish the paperwork on that a little later. Before Mr. Moneyman arrives, so don't worry." Taking a feigned shy, but sincerely infatuated glimpse at Jinn on the bed, where he hadn't so much as moved a muscle, Philip said more softly, with a flicker of a smile on his lovely lips, "Anything else, Val?"

Valdemar's handsome face hardened, and his beautiful, athletic body went all rigid as his gaze bounced back and forth between Philip and Jinn. Undecided, he stood there frowning, trying to find a reason to stay or to delay his departure but too rattled to come up with anything. Jinn wondered in passing why Val's behavior wasn't more amusing to him, even though he found himself unexpectedly very much attracted to Philip. Maybe he wasn't as vindictive in his covetousness as he'd initially surmised—or perhaps he'd taken a liking to Valdemar as well, to the point of not wanting to see him any more miserable than Philip. And the two did like and want each other.

Jinn decided to act as the go-between in this weird lovers' triangle. Wrapping the sheet around his hips tighter, like a robe, he dislodged himself from the bed with a courteous smile. "Pip, I'd like to wash up, if I may. Where might I do that?"

The surprise—and reticent gratitude—on Philip's face rewarded Jinn's effort at matchmaking. "Two tents over. There's a bathing facility, and there should be hot water too." Philip's sunny smile opened up his face in a sweet way Jinn found most endearing, and when the two sexy dimples came out to play along with that tentatively flirtatious smile, he was certain that, regardless of what happened between Pip and Val, Val would have to fight him for Pip's heart.

But… that would be a confrontation for another time. Bowing his head, as was his custom, Jinn took his leave. Bunching the sheet into a wavy ball around his hips, he made his way to the bathing tent. Yes, he wasn't exactly properly attired to make such a public sojourn, but with his imagination he had no trouble coming up with the possibilities of what he'd do if anyone saw him.

And besides… what use was there for clothes when Jinn longed to get naked with Philip? Soon, he promised his libido and heart alike, with a salacious grin of his own as he sauntered toward the bathing tent.

Chapter Three

BARELY containing the rush of steaming hot jealousy—or the boiling hot arousal—within, Valdemar watched Philip wave his hand delicately to indicate where the two of them could sit and talk around the foldable fake wooden table that was covered with books and notebooks, papers, and small artifacts too broken or covered in muck to be taken to the appraisal tent. Silently, Valdemar took his seat, adjusting his position several times, trying to get comfortable, but failing. The truth was he was too emotional to just take it easy.

"So...," he started, a million questions dancing on the tip of his tongue, but feeling more than a little tongue-tied by the mix of emotions—and proper decorum. Unable to look at Philip, Valdemar had to squeeze his hands together to prevent himself from grabbing hold of Philip and never letting go.

"I-is there something you want to ask me...?" Philip asked quietly, but his chin lifted in defiance again, as if challenging Valdemar to comment about what he'd just witnessed. Not that that was any of his business, and with the kind of player reputation Val had, why would someone as sweet, kind, and innocent as Pip be interested in him?

Nonetheless, Valdemar hated how timid Philip could sound with him sometimes, but Val knew he was navigating uncharted waters here. Not forbidden territory, exactly, but certainly not sanctioned, either. But he'd denied his desires for so long that, not only were they unfortunately becoming second nature to him, they were also forcing loneliness upon him. He was driving himself mad with the images of Pip with that… man.

Who the hell was he anyway? And what did he want with Pip? No, Val knew exactly what that god of a man wanted with Pip. That had been painfully obvious, and he growled. Only when he saw Philip's hazel-brown eyes widening in shock did he realize he'd not suppressed the sound quite as effectively as he thought he had.

"I didn't know you had a boyfriend, let alone that he's… here." Attempting to sound nonchalant wasn't working as well as Valdemar would've liked, especially after that grizzly bear session.

Philip frowned, but Valdemar wasn't sure of the reason behind that. The interruption amidst sex, his inquiring question, his mere presence, or all of the above?

"Jinn is…," Philip started but stopped in midsentence, looking more than a little baffled and a lot lost, and Valdemar longed to hold him in his arms but didn't dare. "Jinn just *is*. It's complicated."

Valdemar grunted. "Yes, he's certainly… something." Silencing the depression welling up in his heart, he managed to utter the query, faking abdication. "Are you two… serious?"

All of a sudden Valdemar observed Philip's lips starting to tremble, and those peanut-colored hazel-brown eyes grew moist with a veil of tears. As startled as Valdemar was, he cursed himself for making Philip feel bad, and then he just couldn't help himself anymore.

Grabbing both sides of Philip's face, Valdemar drew Philip close in a flash and kissed him fiercely, crushing their lips together with all the pent-up passion within his heart and body. Feeling those warm, soft lips against his own, he longed to test the seam of

Philip's mouth with his tongue, to open him up, to taste and devour him.

In his dazed state it took Valdemar a moment to fathom that Philip was struggling against him. Ashamed out of his mind, he let go of his never-to-be lover's face and stumbled back to his feet. "I— I'm sorry, Pip... I didn't mean to... I'm so sorry...." Stammering, which he'd never done before and hoped he'd never do again, as it was very uncomfortable, Valdemar was stuck between his instincts to run away and to stay and reassure Philip his intentions were honorable—for the most part. Yes, he'd done a lot of questionable and amoral things in the past, but the one thing he'd never intended to do was to hurt Pip.

Philip's pale face was shocked as he stared at Valdemar, whose hope of being with Philip withered and died right then and there. "B-but... y-you don't like me like... that...." Valdemar was confused beyond belief, and saw the same expression mirrored on Philip's lovely, open face.

Shaking his head, as if that would clear the haze of lack of comprehension, Valdemar mumbled, baffled and incredulous, "What...? Don't want you...? By the gods, Pip, you're *all* I want." Philip's hazel eyes widened more, and his jaw dropped, and Valdemar hastily added, "I didn't think you'd be interested in me, considering my flirtatious Casanova reputation and all, and you being so sweet and perfect and lovely and—"

Without giving Valdemar the chance to add anything else to his impulsive confession, Philip jumped up from his seat and lunged at Valdemar, practically climbing all over him, wrapping his arms and legs around him and kissing him so hard on the mouth that he stole Valdemar's breath away—along with his heart.

Philip tasted like Darjeeling tea with sugar and honey and peanut butter cookies, and to Valdemar these bursts of flavor were the essence of ambrosia. Embracing Philip to his heart and body's content, Valdemar slanted his head to a better angle and deepened the kiss, resorting to using every part of his mouth—lips, tongue, teeth, and breath—to please the guy he'd coveted for so long.

Suddenly there was a sharp bite on his lower lip, and the sting of pain overshadowed the pleasure. Alarmed, Valdemar drew back, brushing the fresh blood from his lips with his fingertips. Philip's hazel eyes had darkened with lust—but with righteous indignation as well.

"How could you think that I didn't... want you, Val?" Philip's voice carried over to Valdemar, bashful and fragile. "When I've spent the whole year—"

"What?" His brain was ill-prepared to handle the information pouring in, and since Philip stopped dead in his tracks, Valdemar guessed that his stunned state showed in his expression as well. "You... *I* am the one who's spent the whole year wishing and pining over you, dreaming of you asleep and awake, every minute of every day, all the time—"

Shaking his head, as if he couldn't understand what was being said—and Philip wasn't alone in that confusion—Philip pressed his body still closer to Valdemar. "No, you must be talking about me. That's what I've been doing."

Though holding each other awfully close, Valdemar gripping Philip's slender shoulders and Philip winding his arms around Valdemar's narrow waist, they stared at one another, flabbergasted, as if across a huge chasm of misunderstandings and misassumptions. But in a rush of consensus, the gap was surpassed, and they gained equal footing.

And just like that, they uttered a laugh in unison and right off began to chuckle, and then the bellows of laughter from deep in their bellies and chest roared out, like a stampeding horde of wild beasts, until they sounded like a couple of cackling hyenas.

Philip buried his face in Valdemar's neck and giggled endlessly. "I-I thought you found me too meager and dull and mundane to ever attract your lustrous attentions."

Valdemar chortled into Philip's sandy light hair that held the scent of apple shampoo. "I believed you'd heard of my less-than-reputable fame as a man-eater and a player, and decided to ignore me, because whenever I looked at you, you looked away—"

Philip shuddered and sucked in a hard breath. "I only did that so I wouldn't embarrass myself by blushing all over and lunging at you and tearing your clothes off then and there."

Licking his lips as his heart skipped several necessary beats, Valdemar thought he'd died and gone to heaven. Closing his eyes, he held Philip tighter against his chest. "I wish you had, Pip. Damn the consequences."

Chuckling, Philip sighed happily, and his arms around Valdemar's waist and back tensed feverishly. "Great, now you tell me." But despite Philip's frantic and stiff reaction, Valdemar heard the humorous attitude in his tone, and felt relieved. But Philip's next statement rescinded that alleviation. "Y-you did flirt with Jinn...." The tone wasn't accusatory but sorrowful, and Valdemar hated hearing it.

So out of the blue a dark storm cloud of doubt rolled in and rained acid fear over him. "This is going to sound really stupid, but I thought that if you saw how charming, tempting, and sexy I could be you'd fall head over heels in love with me on the spot." At that Philip made a disbelieving snort, but his hands tightened once more around Val, so he surmised the crisis had been averted. Yet, there was still left the question of Jinn. "What about that... boyfriend of yours, Pip?" Valdemar still couldn't say his name, and didn't want Philip to ever say it again either.

This time when Philip froze, Valdemar worried he should not have spoken at all, but finally Philip said, "Jinn... Val, I can't leave him." When Philip moved out of his arms, Valdemar saw the love-filled castles in the sky of his dreams come crumbling down and turn to dust. The conflicted look on Philip's face confused him, but he slid his hands down his arms to comfort him as he began to tremble. Whatever was going on between Pip and Jinn, Valdemar would stand at Pip's side through it if he so chose. Shyly Philip muttered, "Val, he's special. And he needs me."

"Who doesn't?" Valdemar mumbled sourly but not as quietly as he'd intended when Philip gave him a reproachful look—but with a tiny twitch of a smile. He hastened to say, "You and I, Pip, we've waited a really, *really* long time get together. I guess I can wait a little while longer. Unless…." He hesitated even speaking the words out of fear that if he did so they'd be true. "Unless… he's the one you want to be with."

The bewildered and slightly desperate gaze Philip shot him filled him with dread. "I need time to sort this out, Val. Can you… will you give me that?"

Unsure again, Philip shivered, his hazel-brown eyes resembling those of a fawn staring up at Valdemar, pleading for understanding. As if Valdemar could've denied him anything. "Anything you want, Pip. Just say the word. Time, space, *him*—you got it."

Sheer bliss opened Philip's haunted face, like the sun breaking through the dark clouds with its brightness and warmth, and his smile spread across his cheerful face, showing off those tiny dimples again that gave Valdemar the hard-on of a lifetime. "Thanks, Val."

Infidelity aside, Valdemar's brain sizzled, and he almost asked Philip if this meant they couldn't make out anymore. But as it was, and despite his reputation that claimed the contrary, he wasn't the type to break up existing relationships. If Jinn was with Pip, Val would steer clear and give them time to resolve matters to their mutual satisfaction. But then again… if Jinn saw even half of that lovely light beneath Philip's unassuming appearance that Val did, he'd end up with a broken heart for his troubles regardless.

And oddly, as much as Valdemar wanted Philip for his own, he didn't want someone else's suffering—not even Jinn's—to be the foundation of his and Pip's relationship. That coldhearted he just couldn't be, no matter how powerful his feelings for Pip were.

Perplexed by his own instincts and emotions, Val allowed himself to attempt an analysis of why he'd feel this way about Jinn, who was, in effect, his rival for Philip's heart. Yes, it hadn't escaped Valdemar's attention that Jinn had purposely left and given him and Pip this chance to talk face to face and one on one. That spoke tons about his chivalrous and honorable character—and here Val was contemplating seducing Jinn's boyfriend. *I guess there was a message there about his character too*, he pondered miserably, and had serious second thoughts.

Aside from his polite and respectable ways, Jinn was also extremely handsome. That Val had not missed either. Val was taller than Pip, but Jinn was taller than either of them. Magnificently imposing and magnetically alluring, Jinn had a sexy, brawny body that just begged to be worshiped in spontaneous and diverse ritualistic sexual offerings. Unable to deny his attraction to that embodiment of masculinity, prowess, and sexuality that Jinn represented, Valdemar's physical reactions were instinctive as waves of arousal washed over him.

What he wanted from Jinn was different from what he needed from Philip—and yet it was similar.

Both Jinn and Pip were desirable men, and Val was a red-blooded man with a healthy libido and a good deal of sexual confidence. As the image of the three of them together sharing a bed popped into his head, Val struggled to free himself of it, knowing that what he felt for Philip he could never feel for Jinn. And a threesome affair where two men loved each other and the third was mere sexual spice could not last beyond the initial high of the newness of the experience. And it was morally reprehensible and ethically unthinkable to engage in an affair where two people meant more than the third.

Valdemar's wild imaginings and ethical considerations came to a dead stop when Philip stepped back into his arms, wrapping his own slender arms around Val's waist, snuggling close and resting his head in the nook of his neck, sighing contentedly.

"I know it wouldn't be fair to Jinn to kiss you again, Val, but I want you to know how much I want that." Philip's timid voice was, despite the underlying emotion, clearly enunciated, as if he meant to be as precise as possible. Looking up at Val, Philip smiled tentatively. "He's an all right guy. Would you give Jinn a chance to prove to you that he's a great guy?"

Giving the boyfriend of the object of his desire an opportunity to keep Philip for himself and force Valdemar out of the picture? Every cell in Val's body cried out a deep-sounding no—but simultaneously every one of his instincts told him firmly the opposite. Valdemar wasn't a mean person, and when he peered into the darkened milk-chocolate-colored, fawn-like eyes of his lover to be, Val would've given the man anything at all.

"Yes, Pip, of course," he replied as politely and honestly as he could muster with the fear of losing Pip before he had even had him clutching his heart with icy cold nails. "I'm sure he's a fine man. If he weren't, you wouldn't have given him the time of day."

Philip scoffed slightly. "If I were such a good judge of character, I should've been able to tell a long time ago how you felt about me. As it is, though, I'm glad the truth finally dawned on me."

Caressing Pip's soft, clean-shaven cheek with its fruity aftershave, Valdemar said—a bit reluctantly but saying it nonetheless, "Just so we're clear, Pip, if you're serious about Jinn and want to have a relationship with him instead, then as much as I want you, I will do nothing to break you guys up."

Philip's smile was at once sweetly grateful and slightly annoyed, and that told Valdemar that Jinn had yet to make his conquest a fully staked claim.

"You two are amazing in your thoughtfulness. Worrying about poor little old me, when you should be kissing until your lips were numb."

Both Valdemar and Philip jumped apart, startled. It was déjà vu all over again, only the players' roles were reversed. Jinn came into the tent from the doorway, letting the flaps close with a small whooshing sound accompanied by the sound of plastic covers meeting. An amused grin was plastered on his handsome, chiseled face as he studied the scene serenely.

Valdemar was more than aware that both he and Pip were staring at the drool-worthy hunk of man with their eyes wide. Jinn had found a pair of light-blue ripped jeans somewhere, and wore them like he had been born into them, the waistband hanging so low on his hips that his toned abs showed to perfection, as did the taut belly, the prominent winglike hip bones, and a sliver of black pubic hairs, taunting the onlookers with promises of sex. Busy toweling his long black hair dry, Jinn smiled wickedly as his electric-blue eyes glanced between Val and Pip.

"So, why aren't the two of you in a continuous lip-lock?" he asked teasingly.

"Jinn...," Philip said, his voice cracking, sounding embarrassed and a little scared.

Dispatching his towel on the back of a chair, Jinn smiled reassuringly—and from Valdemar's perspective, he could've sworn the man aimed the gesture at both of them. "You both want to do it, and I want to see you do it. Besides, denying who you are and what you want won't do either of you, or any of us, any good."

At that point, Valdemar was certain he'd never heard more enticing—and disconcerting—words in his lifetime. And denying the feelings those words evoked within him—for both Pip *and* for Jinn—did enter his mind, but only in passing until... all that was left was desire.

Chapter Four

HIS mind all jumbled and invaded by a heady haze, Philip wasn't sure if he was still breathing normally. His heart was pounding in his chest like a caged animal seeking freedom. And he was striving for that same goal too.

And how crazy was it that when he woke up this morning he'd had no one—and now there were *two* drop-dead gorgeous, sexy-as-sin men competing for his attentions. Yes, it was mad, and overwhelming, and impossible, and....

Pinching his arm so severely there'd be a bruise there the next day, Philip sought actual physical evidence to prove that what was happening around him was indeed real. The sting of pain certainly was, as he made a small whimpering sound as a result.

Looking up, he saw both Valdemar and Jinn staring at him. Val's expression revealed not only the passion he felt, but some unusual shyness as well, and a hint of humor to boot. Jinn, on the other hand, was grinning like the Cheshire cat again, his powerful arms folded across his chest as he watched the scene play out.

As was his awkward custom, Philip blushed so hard the feverish feeling encompassed his whole body, and he felt his cheeks burn as if a fire had been lit beneath his skin.

"Come on, Pip," Jinn cooed amusedly. "You know you want to."

Yes, that Philip could not deny as his eyes shifted to Valdemar, who he'd dreamed of ever since he'd seen the man at an archaeological symposium in London three years earlier, and even more so when they'd started working together a year ago, side by side out here in the middle of nowhere. His breath hitched in his throat and heat flushed his groin.

But what did Val want?

As Philip's hazel eyes met Valdemar's sky-blue eyes, he saw fire, passion, and dark lust there, and he had his answer.

"Pip, I...." Hesitating, Val turned to look at Jinn. "Are *you* sure...?"

Letting out a sound resembling a combined sigh and chuckle, Jinn shook his head with a berating expression and came up to them, placing his palms on the backs of both their necks, and pressed Pip and Val closer until their lips met in a chaste closed-mouth kiss. Even then Philip could still feel Jinn's hand on the nape of his neck, caressing, tugging on the hairs lovingly.

With a shattering moan, Philip gave in to Jinn's encouragement, to Val's tenderness, and to his own passionate need, coursing through his veins like magma. Almost collapsing on Val, Philip wrapped his arms around Val's shoulders, pressing his body closer to Valdemar, who in turn wound his arms around the small of Pip's back, drawing him tight against his own body.

As deeply drawn into the kiss as Philip was, he still heard Jinn's soft, low laugh from his side. "That's it, dear boys," Jinn whispered with a sensuous drawl that sent shivers down Philip's spine, and he felt a similar shudder wrack Val's body. The mimicry of Philip's Oxford English accent only intensified the seductive sensation.

Yet suddenly it was Valdemar who broke the kiss, panting slightly, the golden freckles on his face visible again as the heat within was pushed through his fair skin. Confused, but with a distinct dare, he stared at Jinn. "How can you let me kiss Pip? Because, just so we're clear, if you do give him to me—even it's just for a kiss—I won't relinquish him back to you, or to anyone."

Philip's field of vision blurred as all the blood apparently rushed out of his brain down into his swelling dick, and he had an embarrassing mental image of fainting in front of these two perfect men. "Val...."

Jinn's smile never faded as he inspected all aspects of Valdemar's facial features, so handsome and earnest that Philip couldn't help but fall for him—and simultaneously for Jinn as well. "Pip has always been yours, Val. With or without me in the picture, that fundamental truth is not about to change."

"But you have feelings for him too," Val said respectfully.

Unable to comprehend what was happening with these two men who both desired him, Philip looked at them both in turn. This morning he'd been alone. Now he felt full to the brim with desire and being desired—and yet he faced the very real prospect of losing not just one, but both of them again.

And Jinn's sad smile seemed to confirm as much. "Yes, I admit that. How could I ask you not to deny how you feel, and not reciprocate? I find Pip most adorable—"

"I am not adorable!" Philip cut in, resentful, and surprisingly, Val chuckled.

Jinn continued as if there had been no interruptions. "And sweet and cute—"

"I am not a puppy, and those qualities definitely describe a love-sick puppy more than me!" Philip's tone had risen, and he saw how now both men looked at him, amused. Yet in his heart he knew he wasn't the butt of a joke, per se, but that he was gently being ribbed. How was it that in this Val and Jinn were like two peas in a pod?

"I know exactly what you mean," Val interjected, grinning, directing his words to Jinn. "I love the way he blushes. It's so damn endearing and precious."

"That was the first thing I noticed about Pip too," Jinn remarked, assessing Philip with his electrifying gaze, like a predator anticipating the taste of prime meat. "Made my cock stand up in applause and my blood fire right up."

And, damn, if those comments didn't make Philip's face reheat like an erupting volcano. "Go on like that, and I promise neither of you will—"

His declaration was abruptly cut short when Valdemar pulled him into a heated kiss that left little doubt in Philip's mind that he was being possessively claimed, and he could do naught to stop it. Not that he wanted to either, as Val's taste of tea and crumpets filled his mouth.

When Val's hands landed on his hips, tugging their groins into close quarters, Philip melted against the man he'd dreamt of for far too long for comfort. When he felt a third hand gently coaxing his hips into movement with a slight press on the small of his back, Philip was certain he'd died and gone to heaven—or to gay paradise. Jinn's touch made him quiver from head to toes as Val's tongue was busy doing heavenly—or sinful—things in his mouth.

"Give it to him good, Val," Jinn murmured near Philip's ear, his warm breath stirring the curls of hair around his temple. The jasmine scent of Jinn's hair and the sandalwood smell of his skin drove Philip mad with sensory delight, being poured over his already overloaded senses. Then Philip felt a tongue brush his neck, the teasing tip licking the soft, sensitive spot beneath his ear. The feel of two tongues, one in and another on him, was a novel experience that threatened to make mush of his already short-circuiting brain.

"Mmm…," was Val's incoherent answer to Jinn's suggestion, as his tongue was actively entangling itself around, over, and under Philip's tongue, seemingly everywhere at once. Jinn's hand slipped lower to cup his buttock, giving a light squeeze, causing Philip to moan wantonly. And when Val's right leg slid forward and upward between Pip's thighs, his strong sinewy thigh muscle massaging Pip's balls with every nudge, Pip felt his rationality vanishing into thin air.

These two men in effect owned him, with their physicality, masculinity, and sexuality drowning out any and all opposition within him. Not that there had been much of that to begin with.

Besides, Pip could not object, since his mouth was being devoured and ravaged by the ravenous suctions of tongue, heated puffs of breaths, mild nibbles of teeth, and smooth caresses of lips. He'd spent so much time wondering what kissing Val would be like, and now the reality of it was better than any of the wild imaginings that had played out between his ears.

To spice things up, there was Jinn—the wild card who'd molded a niche for himself within the get-together between Pip and Val. To be honest, Pip had to admit that without Jinn no connection would have formed in the first place. In essence, Pip had Jinn to thank for being in Val's arms right now—and Jinn's presence only added to the sexually volatile situation.

Breaking the kiss so that they could both catch their breath, Val gave Pip a series of featherlight kisses from his lips past his jaw and down to his neck—the other side from Jinn, and just like that, Pip had two sets of lips attached to his neck, both kissing, licking, and suckling like a couple of vampires on a mission to seduce and consume.

"Oh my God...." Pip trembled all over, and his knees felt like they were made of jelly and Silly String instead of bones and muscles. Two pairs of palms stroked his back and hips, first merely lifting the hem of his shirt but then divesting him of it, revealing his luminescent white skin and thin frame with prominent bones and tendons. Extremely self-conscious about his physical differences from the two big and muscular men surrounding him with their bulky bodies and sturdy limbs, Pip shook even more, surrounded by walls of hard, heated flesh.

"Feel his dick, Jinn," Val huffed hoarsely. "Pull it out." Pip barely recognized the fact that Val had spoken Jinn's name for the first time, and he sensed that this first-name familiarity between the two men boded well for sexually strenuous times for him in the near future.

The choked chuckle Jinn made affirmed Pip's belief that he was definitely being outmaneuvered by the two men with the single-minded purpose of getting him in bed—with both of them at once. And Pip absolutely wanted that goal to be reached until Val and Jinn had had him in every conceivable position a hundred times over, and then some more in other locations around the excavation site and then around the world. His imagination was running wild with pornographic reels over and over again, and he gasped as his heart thudded in his chest. These hard muscles, these ripped bodies, these potent grips—Pip wanted more of them. More of Val—and of Jinn.

Jinn's hand slipped under the waistband of his khakis, as it had before, and Pip's cock popped up eager, ready, willing, and able as Val's hands unbuttoned the pants and eased them past his hips down his thighs in a bundle along with his cotton underwear. The desert air was warm, but it felt cool against the feverish skin of his dick, and having Jinn's hand fist it didn't help matters at all.

"Touch it, Val," Jinn urged solemnly. "Take it in your hand. Put it in your mouth."

All possible words, either dissent or approval, in all familiar languages escaped Pip as what was about to happen shook him to the core. Jinn's big palm was rough against his most sensitive, softest skin, and when he felt Val's fingers intertwine with Jinn's, rubbing and gripping, Pip moaned louder than he'd ever dared. But when two mouths latched onto his neck, his moan morphed into a hiss and a purr.

"Sweet sounds, Pip," Val murmured in approval, his breath fanning hot over the wet spots on Pip's neck, giving him chills all over.

The two hands working Pip made him melt into a puddle of lust until his knees gave out and he slumped weakly against the two men. And they were right there for him, catching him, holding him up sandwiched between their rock-hard bodies. "Please...," he pleaded with a raspy tone, swallowing and licking his lips to trying to find some strength to his waning semblance of a voice.

Dizzily, he managed to look down where two hands fondled, stroked, and massaged his cock up and down, squeezing hard and caressing lightly. "I always knew you'd be beautiful, Pip," Val murmured, his gaze also aimed at Pip's dick. "Long, pink, pretty, all cut and wet with your come." Transparent rivulets of precome were indeed dripping down the seven-inch length of Pip's rose-hued dick, and two hands lubricated the shaft with the warm fluid, easing the friction but adding to the outside pressure seeping through and building within him to a boiling point.

"I want to kiss you," Val mumbled breathlessly, his sky-blue eyes hooded in dark lust and his voice emanating from somewhere deep within his core.

Pip looked up, tilted his head, closed his eyes, and parted his lips in anticipation of the imminent kiss.

Only he waited in vain, his eyes shut, as only air met his tingling lips.

Then the tight shape of luscious lips enclosed the twitching head of Pip's dick, and he moaned. Jinn took advantage of his succumbed state and advanced on his lips, covering them and pushing his tongue into the dark, wet heat. Pip wound his left hand backward around Jinn's neck while his right hand wandered and raked through Val's blond hair, which was the color of honey near a fire but also carried the tone of snowy powder in sunlight, with so many various hues that Val's hair alone was always able to mesmerize Pip.

Only now he couldn't see the shade as his eyes were closed and his senses enraptured by Jinn's kiss and Val's kiss—in two different places on his body. Jinn's wide, limber tongue licked his palate and curled around his tongue until Pip was panting into the kiss, unable to get out a word. Val's tongue, just as it had inside his mouth, felt like it was everywhere at once, licking up and down his shaft, encircling the ridge of his crown with a tight ring of his lips and then his tongue, mercilessly teasing the sensitive spot under the ridge and lapping up the dripping precome from the small slit at the top, darting his tongue against it. And around Pip's body there were four hands, caressing, stroking, fondling, gripping, pressing, pulling, digging into skin and flesh, leaving Pip in a state of arousal he had no experience with or a name for.

"God, Jinn, you have to taste this," Val mumbled in front of Pip's prick, which was now sporting a darker shade of pink, closer to fuchsia. Pip could tell since Jinn had let go of his mouth with a wet smacking sound so obscene it titillated him to no end.

Dropping to his knees next to Val, Jinn licked his lips hungrily and immediately enveloped Pip's prick with his mouth, the hot, velvety, greedy suction almost too much for Pip to bear. Faintly, through the roar of blood in his ears, he heard Val chuckle, and as the man, with his striking Viking appearance, stood up and faced him, his pink lips now a darker shade of magenta and swollen wet and plump, Pip almost creamed himself right then and there.

But then Val's lips covered his own, his long tongue delving deep to explore and conquer, and tasting his own come and Val's unique flavor both together on their entwining tongues, Pip wanted nothing more. And then he was proven wrong when Jinn's mouth gorged on his cock like a starving man attacking a piece of meat. Whimpering into Val's kiss, Pip feared it was game over when the fiery tingling gathered in his groin and twisted within his gut.

Breaking the kiss, Pip gasped and uttered with his last strength, "I'm gonna come."

Before he'd even caught his breath, Val had dropped down on his knees again, and just when Pip was certain his brain couldn't fathom and his body couldn't handle any more stimulation, he was again proven incorrect. Val's eager tongue licked around Pip's shaft until it reached the top—and mingled with Jinn's tongue there, both suckling the silky skin, lapping the drops of precome, and licking all around the crown, their tongues entangling in a lewd kiss around Pip's pretty prick until his heart pounded in his chest so hard he almost saw the banging through the skin with his own eyes.

"Oh my God...." These were the last words he was able to produce, and then he was coming, exploding like the fireworks on the Fourth of July. Thick, creamy streams of come erupted from his cock as his emptying, aching balls felt like they were being mangled through the wringer, and the heat and sight of Jinn and Val eating him up were suffused into every fiber of his being until he knew he'd never feel as sated with anyone else but these two men.

As Val parted with Pip's now depleted and utterly spent dick, he said in a gravelly voice, happy as a clam, "I knew it, Pip... I knew you'd taste both salty and sweet."

Both men stood up—and Pip felt like falling down. But Jinn's strong hands held him up as Val cupped Pip's face and kissed him on the lips, giving him a taste of his own sexual flavor. Pip had never felt more weary and energized, more satisfied and hungry, more wanted and wanting.

"I agree," Jinn offered, brushing a kiss over Pip's cheek. "You taste divine."

The compliments made Pip blush all over again. But in the back of his head there was the thought that, while these two perfect men had given him so much pleasure it had melted his brain, he had yet to reciprocate. "D-do you want me to…?" His fumbling hands landed over the groins of both men, his curving fingers feeling how hot, hard, and heavy their cocks were through their clothes—Val's khakis and Jinn's jeans.

Jinn chuckled huskily. "Maybe we should take this to bed before one of us falls flat on their ass?"

"That's not necessarily a bad thing," Val needled, his blue gaze zeroed on Jinn's blue eyes, and Pip had no trouble telling that for these two men this was no longer about separate competition but shared pleasure.

Jinn bowed his head in recognition of the stated fact. "No, not at all." Jinn proceeded to attack Pip's neck with serious intent, biting the soft junction between his neck and shoulder, his teeth nibbling away until Pip gasped in delight—and felt his cock begin to swell and rise again.

Val's lips claiming Pip's lips muffled out the sounds temporarily, and his head was humming and his body buzzing. "I wish I could kiss you forever," Val mumbled heatedly into Pip's mouth, taking his time with gentle teasing of Pip's lips with his own, sensitizing them even more, creating ripples of tingling sensations on Pip's lips. Only once in a while did he feel the tip of that long, nimble tongue licking the curves of his lips in passing, and the light touches were driving Pip insane.

Pip shuddered in passion and purred with the knowledge of being wanted so. "I wish that too…." All of a sudden he grasped what he'd uttered, jerked back as fast as a lightning bolt, and stared Jinn down with a furious glare. "*No!*" He held his finger up firmly in front of him in a manner reminiscent of an old-fashioned schoolteacher who used her ruler to dominate her classroom with fear. He was well aware that he looked ridiculous making the gesture, but he had to confirm to his genie that that had *not* been a wish in any way, shape, or form.

"What…?" Baffled, Val's curious eyes shifted from stern Pip to amused Jinn over and over, obviously not having a clue about what had changed the mood of the situation in the blink of an eye from the wonderful sexual tension to this strenuous commandeering. Pip was aware of that, too, and the fact that two hands were still pressed against his naked dick, and that his own hands covered the sharply straight-up rising dicks of both men. In passing he wondered if some rubbing would get things back on track—and derail Val from his questioning.

"Oh, Jesus, I'm sorry…."

A young, athletic man with short brown hair and a discernible American accent turned away from the tent doorway, embarrassed, as he'd tried to come in while three aroused men were holding each other's cocks. "Didn't mean to… um, interrupt anything."

Val turned his head toward him, quickly dislodging Jinn's grip and tucking Pip's dick back in his pants, buttoning up the fly like a pro, with a quick glance to make sure nothing remained in sight. "It's all right, Ricky. Is something wrong?"

The young man refused to look back inside, and he barely held his face in check as he struggled to suppress the ensuing chuckles within. "Oh, Mr. Moneyman's here. I put him in the dining tent."

Frowning, Val looked at his wristwatch. "He's early."

"It's not the same guy as before, so maybe his schedule is—"

"Keep him there, and please inform him that I'll be there shortly." Val's voice had taken on the professional scholarly and leadership tone Pip had worried would reemerge along with his flirtatious defenses. But the latter shone with their absence as the tone was all business.

"Will do, boss." A small but less than subtle burst of amused laughter exited the confinement of Ricky's throat as he quickly strode off, letting the tent flaps fall back in place, briefly shutting out the outside world.

"Doesn't anyone around here knock?" Pip muttered to himself in frustration, and then he realized Val and Jinn were watching him intently. Despite the closeness and intimacy the three of them had shared not a moment ago, Pip still blushed all over again—though he suspected some of that was due to the lingering effects of sexual release. At least, he hoped so.

Val chuckled, giving that charming smile of the player again. "Pip, I've got to go and meet Mr. Moneybags, and hopefully he'll cough up the dough to keep this place running for a few more years at least. And... give us the time to get to know each other— intimately."

Pip had waited so long to hear these words, and now that he had, he seriously contemplated swooning. "Val...." And then he just didn't know what else to say in his current condition of afterglow— which was funny, since as a scholar and a scientist he lived off putting his knowledge into words on paper.

"We'll continue this later... right, Pip?" Val whispered enticingly, leaning down and kissing Pip tenderly on the lips, and not only did it feel like an invitation to Pip but also like a promise. The warmth flooding him settled in his chest instead of his groin. Nodding, not trusting his voice, Pip kissed the man back. Turning his head ever so slightly, Val looked at Jinn with a similar query. "Right... Jinn?"

Jinn grinned and nodded as well, his long black hair now dry and flopping down in full waist length to frame his chiseled face. "Hurry back." To that, Val's eyebrows lifted in surprise, and then elation curved his beautiful lips into a contented smile, and he added to the triangle of nods.

Ruffling Pip's hair affectionately, Val walked out of the tent, and Pip heard himself exhale loudly, as if he'd been holding a tense breath the whole time—and considering the hot knot in his belly that slowly began to unwind, that might've been the truth.

Pip turned to Jinn warily, worried Jinn would think they'd gone too far as a threesome in their sensual escapade, but once he saw the genie's teasing smile, he relaxed considerably. Jinn chuckled and caressed Pip's hair lovingly, just like Val had done. "Well, Pip... I'd say that went well, wouldn't you?"

Chapter Five

THE dining tent was vacant when Val entered it, and he wondered angrily if the glorified accountant had wandered away just to piss him off. Whoever this guy was that any of the number of organizations funding the expedition had sent had already made the grievous error of rubbing Val the wrong way.

When he could've stayed at Pip's tent and gotten rubbed the right way. The oh, so fucking right way. At least his dick wasn't straining for release through the fly of his khakis anymore, but the annoyed throbbing of getting all worked up and not getting to party was still there. Yes, his cock was furious with him right now, and Val couldn't blame him.

Sighing in frustration, Val went back outside and stood in place, his gaze searching the vast open areas between the many tents around the site. Spotting Ricky going into the storage tent, Val sprang into motion, running after the younger man.

"Hey, Ricky, where's the suit gone off to?" he shouted as he closed in on him.

Ricky turned around upon hearing his name called, his arms filled with an open wooden crate stuffed with broken pottery, and grinned. "Say what now, boss? And here I thought you were the master of finding lost things, not losing them."

"Fuck you." Val stopped in front of him, giving him a scolding stare, but restraining the slap he aimed at the guy's head—in his imagination. "Did you see where he went?"

"No, boss. I forgot all about him." Ricky shrugged. "Maybe he went straight to the retrieval or appraisal tents." Vaguely, he pointed in the general direction between the dining tent and the sleeping tents, not that Val needed reminding where everything was situated. He'd been here for over a year already—a month before the expedition officially kicked off to set the site up, and then just shy a week of a whole year spent excavating more of the mysterious nameless city sprawled below their feet, vast and unknown.

Without saying a word, Val huffed in indignation and strode toward the retrieval tent in a hurry. Everything was well catalogued and brought to the appraisal tent for laboratory testing, scientific evaluations, and precursory theoretical assessment of purpose, function, significance, and so forth. Before that, though, all discovered items they'd collected ended up in the retrieval tent for preliminary inspection and cataloguing. If anyone intended to rob the site, that would be the place to go since it would take time for the expedition members to notice something was missing.

And artifacts retrieved from cities of the formerly Unseen world, whether populated to capacity or abandoned to ruin ages ago, were worth a ton of money on the black market. That's why they typically took digital images of found items immediately before cataloguing, just in case.

Wrenching the flaps of the tent open, Val entered the retrieval tent. Just like he'd surmised, there was a government accountant type perusing the desks filled with artifacts of all shapes and sizes, awaiting inventory. Medium height, stocky under his charcoal gray formal suit, that must've been agony in the scorching afternoon heat of the surrounding desert, the man turned to look at Val as he entered. Unlike most of his peers—and God knows Val had met more than his fair share—he didn't have glasses, slick hair combed back or sloppy hair all over the place, or the bland look on his face his kin sported on regular basis when encountering anything other than the numbers that kindled the flame in their eyes. Instead he had stark dark eyes that inspected him with a kind of professionalism and coolness Val hadn't expected, and his hair was cut so short it was practically a crew cut. Instead of the pudgy, creamy complexion of most of the nerdy office folk, this man had a muscular build, tanned, rough skin, and what even from afar looked like white scars on his stubbled cheeks.

A courteous—but fake—smile graced his lips as he stepped forward and extended his hand in a greeting. "Dr. Valdemar Velde?" Even his voice lacked the shrill tone of those accountants Val had had the misfortune of meeting, sounding calm and composed, if a little raspy, the way chain smokers did. "It's an honor to meet you, sir."

"That's *Professor* Velde," Val corrected icily. Though he didn't normally care which of the many academic titles he held people used, with this man he sought the superiority only expert knowledge of his field and prestige of his office afforded him. "Mr....?"

"Webb, Professor. Harold Webb."

Val grabbed the man's hand, and was again surprised at the strong handshake the man offered. "You're early, Mr. Webb. I was under the impression you weren't due until later this evening."

Webb chuckled slightly, but to Val it sounded more like an amused growl, the kind of sound people made when they were looking down on their conversational partner. "I caught a ride." His assessing gaze landed hard on Val, and narrowed. "There's no problem, is there?" Why was it that the question coming from this man resembled the kind of half-hostile, half-polite query a cop might use?

Val shivered inwardly but kept his tone professional. "Of course not. But we do have a daily work schedule, and unannounced visitations are never welcomed interruptions."

Webb smiled blandly. "I understand, Professor Velde. Let's get this over with expeditiously then, shall we?" Val silently sighed in relief that there was no more small talk forthcoming, but before he could ask the man to follow him to his office tent, Webb continued nonchalantly, "I assume all these artifacts have been properly catalogued, yes?"

Val held back his steaming annoyance at the insinuation they weren't up to the task at hand. "This is the retrieval tent. Cataloguing is done here. Those tables at the back are where the artifacts that have yet to be catalogued are placed, and once that is done they are moved to these tables in the front so that they can easily be taken to the appraisal tent. And as I'm sure you noticed, Mr. Webb, there is a guard placed outside all retrieval, appraisal, laboratory, and storage tents."

Webb gave a courteous nod. "I did observe your impressive setup, Professor Velde. I have no complaints about the effectiveness of your operation here. I'm only interested in the cost aspect, as I'm sure *you* understand." The implication of that statement did not go unnoticed by Val, who gritted his teeth without letting it show outwardly. "The cost of any scientific expedition, of course, is closely tied in with the human equation." Val frowned. He wasn't quite onboard that one. "With that in mind I was wondering if perhaps you could proceed to give me a tour of some of the artifacts you've uncovered in the past few days so I can get a better understanding of your daily recovery process. I've found that that approach gives me invaluable insight into the intricacies of scientific research out in the field—and allows me to better judge the worth of such procedures. I'm sure neither of us wishes this expedition to lose any of its precious funding."

Val suppressed the urge to knock the man's jaw out of alignment. Instead he generated his most charming smile, flashing his white teeth. "I'd be glad to, Mr. Webb. Would you like something to eat before we get started? You've had a long trip, and I—"

Webb raised his palm up steadfastly. "Thank you for your generous offer, Professor. But it is absolutely not necessary. I prefer *not* to work on a full stomach. Dulls the senses, you understand." Waving his hand about in a general, vague manner, he said, "Shall we?"

For the next half hour, Val showed most of the items uncovered from the nameless ruined underground city, demonstrating their recovery processes, explaining the significance of the sight for science and posterity, and giving a detailed account of their daily itinerary. Webb's expression remained blank, but his gray eyes belied the impression as they roamed every artifact with precision, like a hawk.

Along the way something began to nag at Val, but he couldn't catch the instinctive feeling by the tail and get a good look. He felt like there was some insight probing its way out of the primordial ooze of his brain, struggling to get out, but Webb kept his mind too preoccupied to focus properly.

He'd practically shrugged off the nagging subconscious feeling when Webb dropped a tag attached to the handle of a broken pottery cup by brushing his arm against it, and Val kneeled to retrieve it, huffing in irritation.

And that's when his head shifted gears into high alert, and the persistent knock on his consciousness became a battering ram that blew across the threshold with the force of an invading army.

Webb's shoes.

They were made of hardened, waterproof black leather, scruffy and worn, covered in sand, dirt, and grime.

They were military-issue combat boots.

Not what accountants wore, even in the most challenging of climates and outdoor field assignments. Not what any of the previous accountants Val had met had worn.

Swallowing hard, Val controlled the flush of emotions that threatened to wash over him like a tidal wave. His professionalism became the levee to hold back the impending emotional flood, and when he got up his face showed no signs of his distress—though he did feel fear, worry, anger, and even outright fury. "You should be more careful, Mr. Webb. These artifacts are older than any of the current civilizations, and they break easily." He attached the fallen tag back on the cup with a piece of string.

"My apologies, Professor Velde. I shall endeavor to be more cautious in the future." Webb's voice was less apologetic than Val had expected and more vexed than he would've liked. The man's gaze scanned the contents of the tables—and that's when Val's heart jumped in a fit of anxiety.

Webb was searching for a specific artifact.

In a stalwart effort to calm himself down and get the situation under control, he offered, "We've been at this for near an hour. Maybe you'd care to join me for a spot of late lunch or early supper?" Val was aware that if he could just get the man out of the tent he could alert any of the number of guards patrolling the grounds. If he could just get him outside....

Webb turned to face Val, and for a second Val honestly and truly allowed himself to believe the man would agree to his suggestion, and it'd be smooth sailing from there.

But his theory didn't hold water.

Webb's face darkened, his jaw tightened, and his posture changed, amping up for a fight. "Where are the rest of the artifacts you discovered today and yesterday, Professor?" And this time there wasn't a shred of politeness in his tone. This was aggressive, demanding, dangerous, and Val wondered whether he should play dumb, or surrender to the inevitable, or start a fight among all these precious items from the unseen past.

But... these *were* all the artifacts found.

His blood ran cold at the possibility that whatever this man was after had already been swiped by some other sticky fingers. *Damn it*, he cursed. *Could this possibly get any worse?*

There was the rattle of a walkie-talkie, and Webb yanked a small black device from his belt—and Val saw the gun in the holster on his side at the exact same moment as Webb tugged on it and brought the pistol up, aiming the barrel with a silencer straight at Val's face without the slightest hesitation or shiver. This was the hand of a stone-cold professional.

"Have you secured everyone?" Webb asked into the radio, his tone as hard as steel.

"Yes, sir. The guards have been incapacitated and the rest of the staff rounded up in one of the storage tents."

Through the commotion in the background, Val heard Ricky's small, frightened voice asking what was happening and pleading for help. Ricky let out a yelp after Val heard a thud, and he realized the young man had been subdued, probably with the blunt grip of a gun.

Fear overwhelmed him. Val could hold his own in a fight—despite being more a lover than a fighter—but when other people were in peril too, he could do naught but wait to learn what these people wanted. And they did want something, or they'd all be dead by now.

Dead.... Val frowned, and his heart jumped in utter terror as he became horribly aware of what he'd forgotten in all this chaos.

Pip.

Jinn.

They could be anywhere. They could be restrained in the storage tent with the others. Or they could be lying dead on the floor of the sleeping tent. Val had to swallow several times to get some courage up past the lump lodged in his throat, a concrete manifestation of all his fears in one.

No, they had to be all right. They just had to be. The gods and Fate would surely not have given him Pip—and Jinn—now, only to rush them from him into the cold, unfeeling clutches of death.

"Professor? I don't think it would too much to ask for you to grant me your undivided attention." Webb's voice was smooth now, startling Val and chilling him to the bone. Webb enjoyed this, Val understood. Webb was a killer of the highest caliber, through and through. "I asked you a question. Where are the rest?"

Val shook his head, confused and frowning. "I don't understand. Like I've been telling you for the past hour, everything is brought straight here from the city. If something isn't here, it's gone missing—and that doesn't happen—or... it's been stolen. Maybe someone preceded you here." He knew it was a long shot to suggest such a thing, but he was running out of maneuvers—especially with that gun stuck in his face and the fear for the safety of the others gnawing at his gut.

Webb searched the inside pocket of his jacket and dug out a printed picture. "Where is *this* artifact?"

Val's blood ran cold, and his nerves almost got the better of him as he stared numbly at the picture he'd taken with the camera of his cell phone just this morning of the electric blue and gold-trimmed oil lamp—which he'd given to Pip.

But... Pip had told Val he'd taken the lamp here to the retrieval tent. And yet it wasn't here. There were only two possibilities as far as Val could see: one, Pip had brought it here and someone had taken it—which was unlikely since the intended thieves were still here looking for it, and not enough time had passed for two thief crews to both do the nasty; or two, Pip had lied to Val—which he just couldn't find in his heart to believe.

He had no answers to give either to Webb or to himself. Only questions plagued him—and fears of the worst kind.

Chapter Six

"WHO used to inhabit this city?" Pip inquired, wandering aimlessly through the massive underground city that had once been the solid limestone walls of the ninth largest cavern in the world. A lot of things had been different before the Veil had lifted. That was clear to Jinn too as he sauntered alongside Pip.

"Do you *wish* me to tell you?" Jinn teased Pip mercilessly.

"Nice try." Pip laughed, and Jinn could tell he did it in spite of himself. He'd quickly grown accustomed not only to gently poking fun at Pip's delicate sensibilities but to hearing his spontaneous and innocent laugh, seeing him blush all over his cheeks and chest, and feeling his unique young flavor rolling on his tongue. "Do you know the name of this place? And no, still not a wish."

Jinn chuckled but chose to reply nonetheless. "The City of Raining Gardens." Once the whole place had been full of lush vegetation and colorful gardens, wildly running waterfalls and streaming aqueducts. An oasis of cooling waters and comforting shade amidst the arid desert and dry heat reigning aboveground, now all traces erased by merciless time, the remnants visible only through the three air and light shafts through the roof as the ambient light glowed all around.

Pip looked at him in amazed awe, his hazel eyes wide open in enthusiasm and his full lips curved into an eager, sincere smile that made Jinn's toes curl. "Did you used to live here?" It was clear to Jinn that Pip loved this place with its sandstone walls, labyrinthine streets, tall palatial buildings, and wide-open courtyards stretching up as far as the eye could see.

Now it was Jinn's turn to be cryptic, and he grinned wickedly. "No one used to live here permanently, for this was a playground for genies. An amusement park for fun and games, so to speak." Pip looked stumped and confused, so Jinn explained a bit more. "Here genies tested their powers and had fun with them and with each other. The place is riddled with deadly traps and mind-boggling puzzles. It's actually quite a surprise that you haven't accidentally activated any of the hazardous and challenging machinations hidden behind and beneath these walls and structures, in the last ten years."

Pip gasped. "Oh my God... are we in danger?" His hazel eyes darted along the walls of stone the colors of the sun, fire, and blood all mixing together.

Jinn shook his head reassuringly. "Not if we don't enter any of the forbidden areas or inadvertently activate anything that could conceivably kill us." Winking at Pip, Jinn grinned to help the young man relax. "Have no fear, Pip. If we get into trouble, you just make your wish, and I will use my powers to free us." To emphasize his point, he snapped his fingers pompously.

Pip snorted but grinned, at ease again. "So, Jinn... what do people usually wish for?"

"Wealth, success, fame, and sex—the usual," Jinn replied, shrugging impassively.

With a pensive look gracing his delicate features, Pip nodded. Jinn had an inkling about what was going through his mind. This was the watershed moment that separated wish masters into two distinct categories. The first group dove into the deep end without contemplating the consequences in advance, and either learned to swim, or drowned, as their only thought was their own pleasure. The other batch worried intently at all the many possible ways they could unwittingly causing harm by phrasing their wish wrong or asking for the wrong thing, and ended up making careful, cautious wishes that had zero chance of destroying the world. For what it was worth, Jinn was glad and grateful that Pip belonged to the latter set of wish masters.

"Do you want any of those things?" Jinn asked, curious.

Pip pursed his lips, and his brow furrowed in serious meditation. "In this day and age, one is always short of cash.... And being successful in one's chosen field is important for the continuation of one's career.... And one can absolutely always have more sex." Pip shone a bright flash of a smile to Jinn, who liked this free, playful Pip. "I don't know, Jinn. I need to think about it some more."

"As you wish," Jinn said, bowing his head and spreading his arms theatrically, and Pip laughed out loud so hard it almost sounded like hiccups. Jinn longed to hug the young man until his breath caught in his throat and turned to gasps of pleasure.

Instead he offered his hand to Pip, who looked at as though it were the most uniquely wonderful thing in the world, and took it without trepidation. His small hand, with its long fingers, was swallowed up by Jinn's huge hand, and they shared their warmth through touch. Pip's skin was smooth and soft, like velvet, and Jinn thought he might like to hold Pip forever—which for an immortal being like a genie was quite a feat to accomplish and a sign of devotion.

"*Attention!*"

The sharp, harsh voice rang loudly, seemingly emanating from everywhere, startling Jinn as he looked around, confused at the ghostly voice floating in the air as if by magic. Pip said quickly,

"The voice is coming through the speakers attached to portable generators and artificial lights embedded all over to illuminate the site. The speaker system is mainly used for emergencies."

From the look on Pip's face, he either didn't recognize the voice or this didn't happen often. As a genie Jinn was accustomed to absorbing knowledge of the world outside like a sponge sucking in water, and these new machines fascinated him no end. "What amazing magics you possess."

"Attention!" The voice said again, silencing Pip and Jinn completely.

"What on earth...?" Pip muttered, perplexed, looking around. Nonetheless, Pip obligingly waited to hear what emergency was upon them and what instructions were to follow.

"Philip Butler," another voice said through the speakers, this one slick and dripping with enough honey to catch flies. "Listen up, Doctor. I'd hate to repeat myself in such a serious situation."

"Is this normal, Pip?" Jinn asked slowly, starting to get worried.

That emotion was echoed in Pip's expression. "No."

"Dr. Butler, it appears you have something I want, and I have something you want. All of your friends are up here waiting for you. I'm sure as a caring person you wouldn't want to disappoint them by being a no-show. So why don't you come up here and join us like a good little boy, and everyone will live to party another day." It wasn't a question. No, it was a demand with the expectation of being adhered to and complied with.

"Can we talk back to them?" Jinn asked, his wary awareness turning to his former predatory form. His sole responsibility was to his wish master, to his wishes and to his safety. But the thought of Val somewhere at the mercy of these mercenary types did not sit well with him at all.

"Yes, there's a call-back button." Pip rushed over to the nearest portable generator, and above it, on the wall by the huge factory-type lights, was a radio. Pip bushed the button and said, "This is Philip Butler. To whom am I speaking?" Jinn listened in silent admiration at the level tone of Pip's voice but knew it wouldn't last forever because of his strong feelings for Val. The worry he was feeling must've been nearly overpowering, and Jinn touched his shoulder comfortingly. The flicker of a smile Pip offered made them both feel better. Jinn trusted that.

A mild chuckle came through the airwaves, but there was no real humor there. It was a cold and calculated sound. "That doesn't concern you, Dr. Butler. What is important is that you recover the item that seems to be lost—but I'm sure it is someplace safe even as we speak."

Confused, Pip looked at Jinn, who shrugged, mirroring the bewilderment. "Where are the others?"

"Everyone is alive and well. The permanency of that state depends on you, so no more questions, if you please." The owner of this smooth voice sounded in Jinn's ears far older than Pip or Val, educated, with a habit of expecting to be obeyed. All this spoke volumes to Jinn about the wealth, power, and loyalty of men this man commanded, and his fear grew.

"What do you want?" Pip asked, his tone subtler and more considerate. He seemed to have reached the same conclusions about the speaker as Jinn, and Jinn felt pride for his rational side working even under the present uncertain circumstances.

"Earlier today or yesterday a member of your expedition uncovered an oil lamp at the site. It's made of electric-blue metal with gold inlay. Do you know it?"

Pip paled considerably and began to shiver, his hazel eyes wide and scared and pleadingly directed at Jinn, who shared each and every one of Pip's anxieties. The word about the lamp and the genie had already reached the wrong ears, and now they were being hunted. Jinn suspected that once these people got what they were after, they'd eliminate the threat these scientists posed. Pip had not catalogued the lamp for obvious reasons, and no one would know about its existence once it was missing. And the devastating tragedy of dozens of dead scientists from all around the world would gather whatever other attention was left to be had.

"Jinn, what do I do...?" Pip's frightened voice trembled as fiercely as his whole body did, and Jinn positioned himself at his side and took the young man into his arms.

But Jinn didn't get the opportunity to respond before the man on the radio spoke again. "Perhaps you need an incentive to be candid with me, Dr. Butler." There were sounds of a scuffle in the background, some electrical rattle on the line, and then a faint, familiar voice came through with more than a hint of desperation and fear. "Pip...."

Pip nearly fell apart at Val's weak voice, and would have, too, if Jinn hadn't caught him with his muscular arms. "Val...," he whispered, and everything he felt was right there, pouring out of him in shuddery gasps and tears moistening his lovely face. Clutching Jinn's shoulders desperately, Pip kept repeating Val's name, fear manifest in waves of sobs.

"Pip, make a wish."

At Jinn's low words, Pip looked up at him, blinking as if the two of them were speaking different languages. Collecting himself in perceptible increments, Pip nodded and took several deep breaths to calm his nerves. Jinn kept his hand on the small of his back, feeling the light tremors there within the supple curves.

Looking straight into Jinn's electric-blue eyes, Pip licked his dry, quaking lips and said clearly, "I wish Val was here with us. Bring him here safe and sound, Jinn. Unharmed."

Even though Jinn was well aware that if this wish came to pass their enemies would know without a shred of doubt that Pip possessed the magical oil lamp, he had no choice but to fulfill the wish when it was spoken out loud. And he wanted Val safe with them as well, so he silenced his own anxiety.

Snapping his fingers, Jinn stepped back. A warm whoosh of air raised a cloud of dust in the air and blew his long black hair around, blinding him momentarily. And then on the sand-covered stony ground sat a very confused Val, coughing at the dust and sand, his blond hair a mess but his sky-blue eyes sparkling intelligently.

"Oh, Val," Pip shouted with sudden glee as he dropped on his knees in Val's lap—not even noticing the man had his hands bound behind his back—and began to rain kisses all over the man's face, covering lips, cheeks, eyelids, forehead, everything he could reach, and his hands wandered feverishly all over Val's body.

And though tied up, Val tried his best to respond.

Jinn smiled in relief and moved behind Val to dislodge the plastic cuffs around his wrists, releasing him from his confinement. The moment Val was loose from the restraints, he wrapped himself around Pip and smothered him with a swarm of kisses of his own, as if they had not seen each other for months instead of a mere couple of hours.

"Oh, God. Val, I was so worried about you. I thought I'd die." Pip's sighs and gasps were infused with words so rushed they were barely audible or distinguishable. His kisses never stopped until he finally found Val's mouth and latched on so hard the deepening kiss must've bruised Val's lips and practically swallowed his tongue. The two men draped over each other in mixed desperation and relief, and Jinn watched happily, never in his considerably long life feeling more grateful for his genie powers.

Finally, Pip and Val broke the kiss merely to catch their breaths, chuckling softly and lovingly, petting and caressing each other wherever they could easily reach, as if to make sure they were truly both there alive and well. The love they shared was evident in every whispered endearment and sweet touch and tentative smile.

"Are you unharmed, Val?" Jinn asked respectfully and quietly, not wishing to interrupt the reunion of the lovers but wanting to ascertain the man's condition.

Dazed, Val turned to face him, temporarily not even seeing him there, being too overwhelmed by Pip's passionate kisses—and Jinn understood perfectly how that was. Slowly Val recovered his sanity and dared a smile with a curt nod. "Yes, I'm fine." There was a confused look on his face as he frowned and looked around, blinking, but he apparently chose not to ask how he had gotten there in the blink of an eye—not at the moment anyway, since his intoxicated attention veered right back to Pip.

Jinn let out a relieved breath and returned the nod. "Good." Then he couldn't resist anymore, and he leaned over the man who was as blond and brilliant as a midsummer's day, cupped Val's face with his large hands, and kissed him every bit as ardently as Pip had a second ago. He could feel Val's reaction as the man stiffened in shock—but then instinctively responded to the kiss.

Parting with a wide-eyed Val, Jinn grinned. "Just making sure."

"If he wasn't fine before, that mouth-to-mouth resuscitation surely did the trick," Pip murmured at their side, with laughter in his light tone.

What had been a blush of arousal was now an impact of emotional awareness on Val's cheeks as his face relaxed into an easy, leisurely smile. Whatever he felt for Pip, he was beginning to feel for Jinn too—and Val wasn't alone amidst these burgeoning, fervent feelings. "Well... good," Val said huskily, brushing his fingers over Jinn's cheekbone. Watching these two amazing mortal men together with him, Jinn felt like he'd come home.

Only a home was not synonymous with danger. And they were most certainly not out of danger. "Val, who are these men up there?"

The radio rattled on the wall, and Val had no chance to reply. The same smooth voice from before spoke through the machine—but this time his voice lacked all the suave composure he had demonstrated previously. "So, Dr. Butler, now I can see why you had not placed the lamp in the inventory of the retrieval tent. And here I was under the impression that I was the only mercenary around these parts. I'm pleased to find I was in error. However, I am also annoyed. Must I remind you, Dr. Butler, that there are still thirty-six people up here awaiting your decision. And I assure you my patience has its limits."

"How many men of his own does he have up there with him?" Pip asked, concerned, shifting away from Val's lips, his tone and face serious.

Val nodded in recognition of the grave nature of the situation. "At least a dozen, as far as I could tell. Looked like professional mercenaries with a lot of hardware, weapons, and high-tech. They're determined and focused. They're not going to give up." He shook his head furiously. "Fuck. This is all my fault. Right after I found that damned lamp I took a picture of it with my cell phone and sent it to the International Veil Expeditions Foundation's main e-mail address."

"That's standard procedure," Pip confirmed, and he glanced warily in Jinn's direction. Jinn knew Pip was afraid of confessing his involvement in this mess—and hiding the lamp from prying eyes and eager hands—and didn't envy his position of having to come clean to the man he admired and adored.

"Yes," Val admitted, still agitated. "I should've known e-mails can be intercepted and decoded even through passwords, secure lines, and firewalls. Damn it all to hell," he growled in frustration. "And the most irritating fact of all is that the stupid thing they were after wasn't even there in the retrieval tent." And there it was, the questioning gaze aimed at Pip, who trembled like a deer caught in a hunter's sights and knew he was done for. "Pip? What did you do with the lamp?"

Pip's lips quivered and he blinked away tears. "Val... I'm so sorry...."

Val frowned, but it was a concerned, not suspicious expression, and he briefly touched Pip's cheek. "Pip, whatever happened, I'm sure you would never do anything underhanded, or devious, or criminal. But our friends and colleagues above will die if we don't give the lamp to these men. Once they're gone with it we can alert the authorities and—"

"No, Val." Pip pushed the man's hand down firmly, but Jinn could tell his heart was breaking, and he wanted to take him into his arms. But the timing was all wrong. "I can't give them the lamp. I *will not* give it to them. I won't give it to anyone."

The inability to understand what was going on was clearly written all over Val's handsome face as he struggled to make sense of Pip's declaration. "Pip.... You couldn't have.... Did you steal the lamp?"

"You gave it to me!" Pip cried out angrily, defensively, because he must've known his ethical position was precarious. "I didn't steal it. How could you—"

Val stopped him by pressing his hand over Pip's mouth. "I know that. I asked, yes, but in my heart I never believed it. I'm just really confused right now. I don't understand why that one oil lamp is so important to them."

Pip opened his mouth, but no sound came out.

Jinn couldn't take it anymore. He'd sat on the sidelines far too long. "Because of me." Val's baffled eyes turned to him, but Jinn was already on his feet, moving to the radio and pressing the button to speak. "Who do I have the questionable honor of speaking with?"

Silence reigned for an interminable moment. Then…. "Who is this?"

Jinn chuckled, and all the self-confidence of his true nature was present in that tone. "I am the one you seek."

The silence was heavy with expectation and thick with barely held back emotions. Finally the mystery man said, "You may call me Mr. Smith. You should advise your current wish master that if he does not comply with *my* wishes, his friends and colleagues will pay the price for his inaction."

To that, Jinn surprisingly laughed with disdain. "And you should consider that the Veil lifting has had unintended, wide-reaching consequences that have changed the situation considerably. Or did you seriously think that nothing has changed?" Only silence greeted him, so Jinn continued, with a plan forming in his cunning mind. "Did you think it was mere chance that my lamp was placed for safekeeping in this underground city? I guess that makes you the fool."

"Oh my God…," Pip murmured, horrified, on the ground next to flabbergasted Val, and then an unexpected series of colorful curses emerged from his throat—which surprised everyone.

Jinn grinned at them both but spoke to the man above them. "There is a reason for everything my former masters did, and my captivity and concealment here are no different. And here we come to my conditions, so listen up."

"I will not—" the man started to say, irritated, but Jinn cut him off.

"The Veil was all that protected the world from the full power of my kind, and only a pure soul, kind heart—and intelligent mind—could harness my powers and bend me to their will. Or did you really think one mere rub would be enough to claim my obedience now that the Veil has been lifted?" Pip looked confused, so Jinn eased his worries with a conspiratorial wink, and immediately Pip sighed, relieved, and nodded in agreement. Never had Jinn felt more connected with a mortal or a lover than he did with Pip.

"W-what are you saying?" the man asked, and Jinn, Pip, and Val all heard the hesitant apprehension there. Half the battle had just been won.

"Philip Butler has a good soul, a warm heart—and a clever head on his shoulders. He solved the puzzle down in the city and unlocked my hiding place—but this only extends to him. If you wish to claim my loyal services, you have to prove yourself just like Pip unwittingly did." Jinn had zero doubts that if he could coax this man to go along with his plan he and his mercenaries would never know what hit them. "Well, sir. What say you?"

"But Dr. Butler has the lamp, so it's already out." The man delighted in his reasoning, but that didn't last more than a second before Jinn silenced him with his scornful laugh.

"He has made his three wishes, so now the lamp has been returned to its hiding place. This was decreed so by my captors. Butler and his companion are on their own. As for you... if you are deemed worthy, you will earn my gratitude and undying servitude— for the length of three wishes, as per the predetermined contract dictated so since time immemorial. Then and only then will I be yours to command. But... you have to find my lamp first, like Pip did. We'll see if you are as smart as you are ruthless. I have served many such men as you, and I look forward to the mayhem we will unleash upon the world. I will be waiting."

At that Jinn hit his fist on the communication device, smashing it to bits. It was an effective means of terminating the distasteful conversation, and Jinn felt a modicum of pride at his actions. Yes, the communication system was still intact, but at least he'd made his point. And... of course none of that rubbish he'd spewed out had been true in any way, but that really was neither here nor there.

"You...," Val kept saying, his eyes wide and his shaking finger pointing at Jinn. "You are a... a genie...." He sounded breathless, as though his voice emerged from the depths of a frozen lake, drowning and cold.

"Val, I'm—" Pip started, but Val's impatient wave silenced and dismissed him effectively, and Jinn could see how despondent Pip became, his stance slumping and his breathing shallow and wet with pent-up sobs.

Val got up on his feet and stared at Jinn with a mix of emotions flashing across his face, fury and irritation dominating the rest. "You're a genie, and you belong to that damn lamp that these thugs want. You transported me from the tent where I was held captive, so Pip must've made a wish. How could you not tell me?"

Jinn wanted to say that it wasn't his secret to reveal, because Val was angry at Pip but for any number of reasons couldn't yet confront him. "Perhaps we could discuss or argue this matter at length at another time and place."

Without waiting for a reply, Jinn walked away, deeper into the uninhabited mysterious city he knew like the back of his hand. Well, he had known it then, and even then only for the most part. This new modern world was the conundrum for him, and if he lived to tell the tale he'd set out exploring every possible facet of it.

As it was, though, he might not survive till dawn.

Wide streets of sandstone stretched straight and clear before him, and Jinn took a moment to appreciate the sight he was so familiar with. This was, after all, his playground—and those mercenaries with their pompous leader were on their way down here to find a magical oil lamp—Jinn's ruse to rescue thirty-eight people from certain death.

"Time to get this show on the road," Jinn muttered, the unspoken warning apparent in his tone, and he snapped his fingers.

Yes, a bound genie's powers were tied to an artifact and the current wish master. But there was a great deal of leeway extended to him when it came to his and his wish master's survival when faced with impending doom. Not that anyone needed to know that fact. It was a question of interpretation, and if a genie truly believed using his powers was the only way to avoid death, they were considered extenuating circumstances. In any case, he'd know soon enough if he was denied this—because his powers would fail him.

Wish granted.

The electrical power systems shot out spark showers as they shut down one by one, and the underground city was drenched in darkness.

"Jinn?" Pip's frightened voice drifted to his ears.

"No fear, young mortal," Jinn replied calmly. "It is they who need to fear. For I am a genie, and they do not understand who they are playing with."

Another snap of his fingers, and the cavern was illuminated again.

Only… these colored lights were dancing, swirling, and swarming around the empty sand and dust covered halls and corridors like magical fireflies. In their warm, dancing glow, Jinn, Pip, and Val walked through the ruined city. Vaulted cavernous ceilings loomed high above in the shadows, beyond mortal eyes, giving the place a sense of both ominous weight and the solace of air and room around them. Clouds of dust danced in spheres of the magical floating lights, but they hid nothing of the underground city, partially constructed of stone and partly cut out of hewn stone.

Only the stone walls, streets, and pillars remained. All the wood had rotted and disappeared long ago, and Jinn felt a twinge of rueful longing. There'd been a time when these halls, courts, rooms, and houses had been filled with bustling activity and jesting laughter echoing from the thick, sturdy walls, and Jinn missed those times.

He knew there was no going back—not even if a wish master ordered him to return to those glorious days of play, fun, and companionship.

Feeling sad, Jinn started when Pip's small hand touched his bigger hand, interlaced their fingers, squeezed gently, and then parted with his empathy for Jinn—despite his own sadness. He gave Pip a smile and felt like he wasn't alone after all. Behind him, he felt Val's fiery gaze aimed at their backs as clearly as if he'd been facing him head-on, but now was not the time to clear the air.

They'd entered the city through the Great Gate of Cascading Light, a massive structure of colossal stone pylons with an archway above carved with pictographic inscriptions. This Great Gate opened to the Majlis al Jinn cave chamber, which before the Great Unveiling had been devoid of visible passageways from the cavern, even though there had been such routes once due to the running water, now dried up. The base of the single cavern chamber of Majlis al Jinn was a dry lake bed that experienced periodic flooding waters from rain through the three roof openings.

From the Great Gate, they'd used the inclining Great Stairway to walk down the shallow steps into the city proper, where the ground level was about a dozen meters below the cavern floor. They had ended their descent around the Great Fountain of Shimmering Pools, a vast circular courtyard with a crystal-shaped fountainhead and a pool shaped like a lotus blossom in the middle—the former now crumbled into rubble and the latter empty and cracked. Their steps echoed all around them here, at the heart of the city of genies, and when the fountain and the number of aqueducts leading away from it had been flowing with crystal clear water, it was like there had been music in the air, Jinn reminisced, melancholy.

From the Great Gate and through the Great Fountain ran the Great Processional Way of Feasts, ending finally far away, at the other edge of the city, where the Theater of Great Celebrations and the Great Golden Palace of the Jinn stood old as time itself, surrounded by the Sacred Grove of Abundance. Jinn remembered dancing, singing, and drinking with the processions along the crowd-filled streets, loving the mix of lanterns, fire bowls, magic dancing lights, and light wells illuminating the city, showing their origins as fire elementals in so many ways it boggled his mind at times. Back then the fires blazing had seemed unceasing, undying, inextinguishable—but nothing lasted forever. Not even the great civilization of the jinn.

Beyond the Great Fountain lay the City of Raining Gardens, the streets, alleyways, and corridors spreading all around them like spokes of a wheel or rays of the sun from this central area, the layout symmetrical and proportional. A similar pattern existed on the other edge of the city where the Palace and the Theater were. Now the entire site was littered with garish orange cones and orange-black roadblocks to prevent access to certain areas deemed hazardous or that remained as yet unexplored. After ten years of on-site research, it was undoubtedly more the former than the latter. Equally gaudy signposts were placed at intersections and street junctures to indicate where specific places had been identified, such as craftsmen's workshops, administrative offices, entertainment locations, ceremonial spaces, and residential neighborhoods. Jinn could see that much of the city had been explored, discovered, and given at least a cursory inspection, but he also knew there was much more to find beyond the obvious and beneath the surface.

With experience and confidence, Jinn led Pip and Val away from the Great Fountain toward the path that led to the Sunken Garden, far off the Processional Way. The copses and groves there had once been lush and green, and the scent of grass, flowers, trees, and fresh water had complemented the smell of men's arousal, filling Jinn's sense memory with erotic imagery of all kinds. After a long day playing in the mazes beneath the city, this green haven, teeming with both riches of nature and pleasures of fleshy companionship had been solace from a primitive, hectic world where great power was the beginning of one's journey and not the end. Humanity had barely crawled out of their caves then, and genies had dominated this landscape beyond the Veil.

Since then not much had changed in the human world at large.

However, Jinn was not greeted with the sprinkling melodies of waters running in the aqueducts or the tender, fleeting scents of blooming flowers and ripe fruits from the fruit trees. The Sunken Garden lay in ruin, forgotten by time and rediscovered by greedy mortals. The precious metals and jewels embedded in the stones and mortar had been dug out, or excavated, as Pip and his peers called it, or plundered, as Jinn saw it. He was only glad that at least genies died in a burst of light, heat, and flame, and as such their nonexistent gravesites and mausoleums could not be scavenged or desecrated.

Jinn felt anger boil up in his heart, and he had to consciously quell the vehement gale threatening the serene pool of his soul.

"I'm so sorry, Jinn." Pip's sympathetic whisper reached his ears, and the soft hand against his palm gripped a little tighter.

Even as Jinn looked with moist eyes at the terraced enclosure surrounded by broken pillars, where only dead trees and empty flower beds welcomed him back home, he knew there was no going home—even if he had not been made a bound genie as punishment for his lascivious indiscretions. He had outstayed his welcome a long time ago, and the memory of his rebellious disregard for rules and codes of conduct rose fresh in his mind.

He still managed to reply quietly, "Thank you, Pip."

"Was this your home?"

Jinn smiled sorrowfully. "No. But here, in an oasis of delights amidst an arid world, I found a place to call a home. Here I had friends and lovers. And here I behaved badly and lost everything I held dear. It's funny how I learned what I valued most only after I no longer had it." Frowning, he was aware they didn't have time for a mournful trip down memory lane, but he couldn't suppress the self-deprecating thoughts ravaging his self-confidence.

"Jinn, please, don't despair. We need you."

Pip's small, fragile voice awoke Jinn from his dispirited reverie, and he shrugged off the blue mood as if discarding displeasing clothes. Now was not the time for these glum sentiments because these two men needed him.

Guiding skittish Pip and grumpy Val past two stone columns depicting lilies, roses, and orchids in engravings on the creamy sandstone surface, Jinn led them down another flight of stairs, the stone slabs cracked and making a deep rumbling noise when they stepped on them. Still, they made the sojourn to the foot of the stairs uneventfully and thanked whatever gods each revered.

From there Jinn made his way through labyrinthine smaller streets and back alleys, and he knew Pip and Val were lost. That had been Jinn's goal from the start as he'd veered them off the beaten path. The Veil lifting had caused problems as far as available information was concerned, and this place where Jinn was taking them should remain undiscovered for a while longer.

They stopped in front of a wall at the end of a street that looked like a dead end. Pip and Val looked around, bewildered and curious, their questioning eyes aimed at Jinn, who smiled in response. "I assume you've at least attempted to decipher the ideograms and pictograms around the city, yes?"

"Of course," Val replied, sounding insulted.

Jinn shrugged impassively at his tone. "And what have you learned?"

"You want to talk about our research results now?" Val asked, incredulous and vexed.

Jinn snorted. "Have you seen these before?" He pointed behind him at the wall constructed of stone blocks fitting against each other perfectly, and a number of hieroglyphics were engraved into several rows of various blocks, seemingly without a pattern.

"Yes." Pip nodded, studying the wall with an enthusiastic curiosity that no danger could apparently dampen. "They are placed all over the city in stone slabs and monoliths, embedded into the walls, written above archways, and even depicted on thresholds. The frequency of their appearance suggests it's more than artistic expression. It is writing, isn't it?"

"You haven't yet interpreted them then, have you?" Jinn asked. Glad that at least certain aspects of his culture remained hidden from these scholarly scavengers, Jinn reproached himself for his thoughts. Pip was absolutely not in this line of work for riches or glory. His natural curiosity drove him forward to ask questions and relish the existence of puzzles, diversity, and places like this City of Raining Gardens. Val, on the other hand... his motives were more difficult to determine.

"I hate to interrupt this fascinating piece of academic discussion, but there are big men with big guns after us. Could we postpone this, I don't know, until we get out of here with our skins intact?" Val's mood had not improved, and Pip's reaction reflected that, which in turn made Jinn mad—and the cycle of negative emotions was ready to keep on spinning.

Not waiting to hear any kind of reply, Jinn snapped his fingers—and his feet parted from the floor as he glided up toward the highest engravings on the wall.

"Oh my God...." Pip's enthralled whisper was filled with awe. "Val, can you see that? He's... he's really... levitating...." Briefly, Val forgot his anger, too, because he stared at Jinn floating high above ground with his jaw hanging open, sky-blue eyes wide, flabbergasted.

Jinn grinned and winked back at the young man. "Don't look so surprised. I *am* a genie, after all."

On top of the wall, he found the right stone block with the glyph of warning stamped on it. With determination Jinn pressed it, and immediately it sunk into the wall until a small, almost inaudible click sounded.

A section of the wall drew back, accompanied by the noise of grinding stones and the rasp of gritting sand. A gust of icy air blew back in their faces from the pitch-black opening before them.

Landing on his feet on the ground, Jinn turned to the other two and spoke his warning: "Abandon all hope ye who enter here."

Chapter Seven

DISTRAUGHT over everything that had gone down recently but attempting to control his many fears, Pip followed Jinn into the dark opening, where cold, stale air met them in a gust of wind, and he sneezed loudly before wiping his nose on his sleeve. Stupid allergies, he cursed himself, remembering in all this commotion he'd forgotten to take his daily dose of antihistamines. Praying they wouldn't get any worse, Pip placed his steps cautiously behind the gigantic genie, who descended the stairs before them with familiar ease.

"You all right, Pip?" Jinn's concerned voice inquired, and right away he felt better, safer, more secure, almost without a care in the world. But then images of dangerous men—and a disappointed Val—behind him reminded him that he was far removed from pleasant normalcy.

"Where are we going?" Val asked behind Pip, but Pip knew he'd directed his words to Jinn. Afraid suddenly that Val would never speak to him again, Pip stifled a sob.

"First stop—Hall of Merciful Waters," Jinn replied, his voice soft for a reason Pip didn't understand. Was Jinn placating them or preparing them for a fate worse than death, as you'd soothe a distressed animal? Not that death in itself wasn't bad enough. In any case, it didn't matter, since wherever they were going, that at least gave them hope. Behind the closed-off secret door, human hunters lay in wait—and there was no hope with them.

Vaguely, in passing, he observed that the sandstone prevalent above in the City of Raining Gardens had changed to sand-hued limestone, but without any evidence to substantiate any sort of conjecture or validate any kind of theories, wondering about that served little purpose for Pip at the present. Limestone was common enough in these parts of the world, and the Great Pyramid in Giza was made of the material.

After what seemed like a mile-long descent in the dark, keeping one steadying hand on the cold stone wall at all times, they reached the bottom. Pip felt passage junctions all around, but Jinn kept moving with the determination and confidence of a traveler treading familiar ground, and instinctively Pip fisted the back of the skintight white T-shirt Jinn had found at the campsite. He needed the support for this blind groping and stumbling in the darkness.

Reaching behind him—before he'd even thought it through— Pip offered his hand to Val. "Take my hand, Val." Only air met his scrabbling hand.

"I'm fine," Val said tersely, and all of a sudden the coldness of the underground passage was nothing to Pip, compared to the icy demeanor of the man he'd held in his arms and kissed like his life depended on it no more than an hour ago. Swallowing the weight of sorrow and depression down past the lump in his throat as best he could, Pip let his hand fall.

Finally, a hint of light began to grant shades of gray to the black void around them, and Jinn led them to a huge round room with a round pedestal in the middle with two different-sized clay jugs. Even though the chamber was poorly and dimly lit, with a cool phosphorescent glow emanating from a few of the stones on the walls, Pip leaned over and studied the earthenware pots with their glazed textures of warm earthy tones. It was as if time had gracefully chosen to leave them untouched.

"Beautiful…," he admired dreamily. "Val, come take a look at these."

His enthusiasm dropped to an all-time low along with his sunken heart when Val said curtly, "This is hardly the time for that. We need to get out of here and alert the authorities." Turning to Jinn, Val asked, "Well, genie? What now?"

Val's hostility didn't go unnoticed by Jinn either, and Pip felt bad for him. It was Pip's fault they were in this mess, while Jinn had done nothing but be trapped inside a magically cursed oil lamp for centuries.

But Pip had no chance to intervene on Jinn's behalf as the man spoke up on his own. "Your attitude is beginning to irk me."

Val scoffed, indignant and dripping sarcasm. "Oh, I'm sorry. Almost getting killed has that effect on me, just like being lied to." He glanced over at Pip, and it was far from a warm, sensuous look.

"At least Pip confided his secret to you, and he felt bad about it the whole time he couldn't tell you. Quite unlike you, I might add." Jinn's tone was harsh and accusatory.

"What the hell is that supposed to mean?" Val spat out, trembling with frustration and anger, his hands fisted at his side.

"You know what I mean, *Váli*."

As if engaged in a silent game of chicken, Jinn and Val stood in place like statues and glared at each other with fury and distrust, and Pip had no idea what was going on. Since their sensual encounter earlier today, he'd hoped he would never again be made to feel like the outsider, even at the risk of them getting mad at him, but here he was again, watching helplessly as the world spun around him and people discussed important matters without him.

"How long have you known?" Val asked, his tone having dropped several octaves, and the gleam in his eyes promised nothing good.

Jinn sighed and put his hands on his hips, appearing the very epitome of mountain-like serenity. "From the moment you found me kissing Pip. You didn't hide your feelings then. Or your true nature."

Val blinked, for a moment looking like he was about to charge and launch himself at Jinn. But then he let out a long, tired breath, staring down at his feet. He seemed at a loss for words, and just kept swallowing, blinking, and shifting his weight from one foot to another. Finally he looked up, his remorseful gaze pointed at Pip, who felt a chill. How much more blame could he take from this man he was so in love with it hurt?

"Pip, I'm… I'm sorry. I shouldn't have accused you of not telling me the truth. With Jinn here, and those guys topside, I do understand why you kept it from me. I'm sorry I treated you badly. You didn't deserve it. Not any of it. Please, forgive me."

The tremors within Pip came from uncertainty and fear, but even if he got another kick in the gut and his heart broken he couldn't deny or fight what he felt for Val. Scurrying across the chamber in a whoosh, Pip slammed into Val and let himself be pulled into a hearty embrace that took his breath away.

"Val, I'm sorry. Forgive me…," he mumbled nearly incomprehensibly into Val's chest.

"No, Pip, I'm at fault here, not you," Val assured him, stroking his back and the nape of his neck gently, whispering lovingly in his ear, blowing warm puffs of air on his skin. "You are so precious to me, Pip. You have no idea."

Pip tightened his hold around Val's waist, and the man reciprocated until their hold on each other led to near simultaneous suffocation. "I love you, Val." The blurted words exited without conscious control, and Pip froze stiff, caught somewhere in the maelstrom of indecision whether to retract or affirm his declaration.

The decision was made for him. "Oh, Pip, I love you too," Val sighed happily, swaying with Pip in his arms. Never had Pip felt happier, and his heart was singing and soaring, dancing and floating.

The next words spoken dropped him right back on terra firma. "I hate to break up this tender moment, but our predicament has not changed." As always, Jinn's cool, composed voice was like a steady rock amidst chaos.

Letting go of Pip, Val faced Jinn with an apologetic, sheepish expression. "Jinn, I—"

Jinn chuckled compassionately. "Hold that thought. Now... sooner or later the men out there will come in here, and by then we should be somewhere else."

"You said this place was a playground for genies," Pip said, reminding Jinn of his earlier statement. "Can't you use your powers to whisk us away?"

Jinn winked. "Only if you wish it."

"Right...." Pip nodded. "I still have one wish left."

"But you said Pip had already used up all his wishes," Val cut in, confused.

Jinn laughed. "I lied. However...." He looked at Pip in earnest. "There's no need for you to use up your last wish on account of our situation, which is far from desperate." Suddenly Jinn looked decidedly uncomfortable and embarrassed, and cleared his throat. "And, uh... how should I put this? Um, here I... sort of... kind of... in a manner of speaking... down here I have... no powers."

"You... have... *no*... powers...?" Pip repeated, sure his brain had malfunctioned.

"Could you run that by us again?" Val asked, frowning, equally flabbergasted.

Jinn coughed again, his electric-blue gaze darting around, avoiding Pip and Val as best he could. "Well, the gist of this place is… this *is* a playground for genies. But once a genie enters the maze and the machines start up, the whole point of this place is that we solve problems *without* resorting to our powers. We're supposed to use our other assets, like intelligence, reasoning, problem-solving abilities, and our physical skills—strength and prowess, agility and speed."

Realization dawned on Pip, and he took a breath. "I see. So, that's why this city is, as you said, riddled with deadly traps and such."

"What's that?" Val interjected, staring at both Jinn and Pip with the same infuriated disbelief. "Wait a second. Back up. Are you telling me that to escape those guys with guns we're now lost in a booby-trapped maze with nothing to help us beside our wits and running feet? Talk about frying pans and fires, Jinn."

Dejected, Jinn said, "The City of Raining Gardens was designed to provide us genies with both challenges and rewards. I do know this place, and I honestly believed we were better off in here than out there." Despite his crestfallen state, he stared at Val, nonplussed. "Can't you use *your* powers to get us out of here?"

"What do you mean *his* powers?" Pip asked in the middle of confusion that seemed to be becoming his natural condition. "Val's not a genie." When he saw Jinn and Val exchange furtive, wary glances, the shock he felt was unimaginable. Staring at Val in abject horror, he stuttered, "A-are you…?"

Val closed his eyes and raked a hand through his blond hair, and Pip felt his heart skip a beat or two. Opening his sky-blue eyes and licking his lips to buy time, Val seemed to choose his words carefully. "I'm not a jinn like Jinn. But… I *am* a kind of… spirit."

Pip's mind shut down and nothing intelligible emerged from his mouth, which was hanging open like that of a drooling village idiot. "A long, long time ago I was known by a different name. Váli. I was a...." Val took a deep agonizing breath and let it out slowly. "I was a lesser god in the Norse pantheon. My brother was Baldur, the god of love."

Pip stared, and even though he did hear the confession, it didn't register or sink in. He had no idea what Val was saying. It was as if he was using words belonging to a different language, or his brain had suddenly shrunk to the size of a peanut. "I... I don't.... What...?"

Placing his hand tentatively on Pip's shoulder, Val began his story. "My brother, Baldur, was the one people knew and loved, and he loved them back in kind. He was a good man and a powerful god. We were prophesized to survive Ragnarök, the end of the world as we knew it. As the world changed and mortals grew in knowledge and number, we gods went into hiding, or traveled to other places beyond this world, or lay down, died, and were reincarnated in human form. But... I was given a personal prophecy that I would find no solace without mortal companionship. And so I was offered a choice to journey far from here or to stay behind and seek out this one person who'd speak to my heart." Val's eyes warmed, and he smiled a little as he caressed Pip's cheek. "It's you, Pip. It's always been you. I've waited my whole life to be with you."

"Me...?" Pip stammered, his heart practically pounding its way out of his chest. Of all the things he'd feared Val would confess, this was absolutely not among them.

"Yes, you, Pip," Val affirmed with a nod. "I felt a ripple of sparks and life go through me when you were born, and since then I've waited a long time to be with you. A lifetime. Several lifetimes, all in all, to be exact."

Pip's voice shattered, and his hand rose to cover his trembling mouth. "Oh my God...."

Val chuckled a bit. "Sadly, no. Alas, I'm not a god anymore. I was raised to avenge the death of my brother, and protection seemed like the natural role for me, so I took that charge of you upon myself when I stayed behind for you, Pip."

"For me...." Pip sobbed. "You abandoned your family because of me...."

Suddenly Val leaned down and kissed Pip on the lips, softly, sweetly, like a promise and comfort. "Nothing and no one of the mythical world has been lost, Pip. The Unveiling made sure of that. So cast off your fears and woes, for I would have given up the world to be with you. And that has not changed." Val pulled Pip into his arms again, and Pip went willingly, melting into the embrace of a man who'd once been a god. "When I chose to remain behind for the chance to be with you, Pip, though you were not yet born, I was given a new role. No longer a god, but a spirit much like Jinn here. A bonded spirit. The only difference is that he serves his punishment via the intermediary of the oil lamp, while I'm bound to you by choice."

"Long ago mortals had companion genies that traveled with them in their mundane lives," Jinn picked up the storyline where Val left off. "Not all mortals, mind you. Only those who were special enough to attract the attention of a genie. There were many reasons for this joining. Mortality forces humans to live with a passion as they know they will not live forever. That drive is very tempting to genies, and some of us chose to become personal genies. I did not, however, as this position was very much thrust upon me without my consent."

"I'm one of these bonded spirits, Pip. Only a Norse one, unlike Jinn here," Val continued when Jinn grew silent. "You are special, the one I was always meant to be with. That is not, however, why I love you. But it is an explanation for why I chose the same career as you, why we met at the conference three years ago, and why I made certain that you'd be a part of this expedition. I wanted to be near you—even if I could never win your heart. It was too much to hope for, as I did indulge in many… uh, sexually… wicked games over the years with people who weren't you."

Pip chuckled into Val's chest as the pieces of the curious puzzle fell into place—and he'd found his place, exactly where he was right now. In Val's arms, loving and being loved by him. "Yes, well, if your brother was the god of love, I guess that explains how you turned out such a hound dog, huh?" He was teasing mercilessly, and when Val laughed and hugged the breath out of him, Pip knew he was where he belonged.

Well, sort of. A deadly labyrinth in the darkness underneath an underground city was *not* home.

Jinn seemed to read his mind, and for a moment Pip wondered if he in fact did. "Well, now that that's sorted, the question remains. Do you, Val, have powers that could—"

Val shook his head gravely. "No, I left all that behind. My only power is immortality, and now that I have Pip, I'll not have that anymore, either."

"What?" Pip parted from Val in shock.

"Later, you two," Jinn warned them in all seriousness. "Unless there's anything else you have yet to disclose?" Jinn's amused and feigned stern stare shifted from Val to Pip and back again.

"Oh, no, don't even think of looking at me," Pip exclaimed, glancing at both men. "I'm the only mortal around here, and Jinn is a genie and Val is a god. I think whatever little boring tidbits I have yet to reveal about my humdrum life pale in comparison, don't you?" Yes, he did have one more secret to keep from Val—the oil lamp on his key chain—but it didn't seem important now. What mattered was their survival, and if Val was captured again, the less he knew, the better.

"*Former* god," Val corrected, but an amused smile twitched the corners of his lips. "Is he not adorable when he gets all flustered, Jinn?"

His gaze raking over Pip's body, Jinn said, "I wholeheartedly agree, Val."

Pip's mood was akin to that of a storm cloud, the rumbling of pent-up emotions preceding the lightning flash of his sharp tongue. "Seriously? Right now? Come on!" His cheeks heating, Pip was going to speak again, but was interrupted.

The round opening they'd used to enter the chamber known as the Hall of Merciful Waters closed with a deep thundering sound. A large stone wheel cut off their only means of escape amidst a stony rumble, and then only dead silence greeted them.

"What...?" Val called out, upset at the suddenness of it, mirroring Pip's feelings down to a tee as he hurried to the closed stone wheel and inspected it quickly to determine if it really was as firmly shut as it appeared. Even from afar Pip could tell that it was, and Val soon stopped, apparently having come to the same conclusion, and returned to Pip's side.

Jinn looked up, but in actuality he was listening intently. "Our pursuers must've triggered something—" His explanation was followed a terrified scream, muffled by the thickness of the walls and the distance in between. The cry of death was cut off sharply, and then again there was only silence. "Make that definitely triggered a trap. A deadly one."

"Are you sure those men will find the secret entrance?" Val inquired hastily. "What's left of their little gang will now undoubtedly be more inclined than before to catch us."

Jinn nodded grimly. "Yes, I'm sure. That one—or another one. This challenge given to genies is worth nothing if we have all the time in the world to think things through. We are immortal, after all. So hunters are allowed entry into the maze to motivate swiftness in tests of rationality and skill, and to pursue genies like me. To chase *us*."

"Wonderful...," Val murmured in frustration.

"Val, that's not helping," Pip said quietly, and both men turned to him. "Jinn has done nothing but help us. He's trying. Aren't we all?" Val opened his mouth to speak, but Pip beat him to it. "Jinn, I don't see any other exits. Are we stuck here now?"

Jinn shook his head, and his long black hair danced around him, the faint fragrance of jasmine flowers reaching Pip's nostrils. "No place in this maze is a dead end. Not even the ones that look like it. Expediency, resolve, and problem-solving are key here." His meaningful gaze landed at the altar-like pedestal carved out of blue stone with the two jugs on top.

Pip followed his gaze. "So, every chamber that at first glance seems like an impasse really isn't, and whatever's in the room is the solution to the puzzle of how to proceed?" When Jinn merely nodded in reply, bowing his head in acknowledgement, his eyes burning, Pip felt like a hero for figuring it out—even if it was obvious. With professional eyes, he studied the altar made of blue stone, the surface so smooth and the texture so silky that it appeared almost translucent, like a membrane of water. Going around the pedestal on his knees, Pip found carvings of a fluid, wavy-patterned writing he didn't recognize. "Jinn, is this writing? What does it say?"

Jinn and Val both knelt next to him to study the finding, but from the baffled expression Val was sporting, he didn't know the language either. Jinn, however, did. *"Out of three and five become four."*

Val and Pip stared first at Jinn, dumbfounded, then exchanged glances with each other, just as confused. "Are you sure that's what it says?" Val demanded, his tone more tense. "Because that doesn't make a lick of sense at—"

Suddenly the whole chamber shook, as if the earth moved beneath their feet, and all three men got up in a heartbeat. Echoes of great machines starting up came from all around them, and Pip almost wished for the unbearable silence to return.

And then tiny round holes appeared low on the walls, just an inch or so above the floor as stony *chuck* sounds accompanied the sequenced openings. Whatever had sealed them before had now moved aside, and small gaps of blackness gaped at them, oozing unknown dangers.

Water began to pour into the chamber from the little holes, the level rising fast.

"Oh my God," Pip cried out, more startled than afraid. The water wasn't icy, but it was cold, and in the time it took them to take less than a dozen breaths, the water level within the sealed room had risen up to their ankles. "Jinn, what do we do?"

"Decipher the riddle," was Jinn's straightforward yet slightly alarmed response. He might have been a genie, but Pip doubted he was indestructible, and now he had charges to protect.

Pip immediately turned his attention back to the pedestal and the two different-sized earthenware jugs sitting on top of it.

Val scoffed, shaking his head, his mood somewhere between amused and bemused, lifting his traveling boots-covered feet that withstood water only so much. "You genies sure know how to have a good time," he exclaimed, his stare at Jinn decidedly scolding.

Jinn pointed a finger at the man and stated calmly, though a bit comically, "Oh, I'm so sorry, poor little Váli, it can't all be bonny Valkyries and rowdy drunken brawls in the great halls of Valhalla with beers passed around, raw meat carried to you to sate your hunger, and songs of heroic deeds to pass the time."

"Oh, is that so?" Val replied, equally taunting with his challenging tone. "I suppose you would prefer to just snap your fingers and magically conjure up a few voluptuous belly dancers reeking of floral perfume or to engage in depraved sexual practices behind the walls of the harem. At least we poor little Viking gods, as opposed to you Veiled genies, know the difference between having fun and getting our asses kicked!"

Jinn stepped right up to Val, and they glared and growled at each other like wild beasts in a territorial match. "You're the one to talk, petty little god-prince, when you were dumb enough to relinquish all your divine powers for a boy who's too good for you anyway!"

Drawing in a sharp, angry breath, Val pulled his fisted hand back, and, snarling, Jinn did the same, both itching for a fight.

"*Gentlemen!* And I use the term in its loosest possible sense...," Pip shouted, and both men turned again to face him. This was getting predictable and tedious, Pip thought, and suddenly he found himself in the position of the voice of reason between a genie and a god. And how ridiculous was that? "Could we please focus and solve the problem at hand before we all drown?"

By then the water level had reached their knees.

"I'm sorry, Pip," Val murmured, ashamed, and he gave a docile, humble look at Jinn, who nodded meekly in agreement.

"I'd be overjoyed if you two *children* could at least pretend to behave like adults for two bleeding seconds," Pip reprimanded them, "because I think I've figured this out." As Val and Jinn, who both shared the same admiring and awestruck expression, approached the pedestal, Pip pointed at the jugs. "I think—and let me remind you I'm not a hundred percent sure on this one—that these two vessels are for two amounts, three and five, maybe liters or gallons, I don't know. But I do believe that's what they are."

"So?" Val asked, bewildered.

Pip smiled a little—even though the cool water was now at midthigh. "I think we have to fill one of these with four liters or gallons or whatnot." Jinn and Val stared at him blankly, waiting. "That's the puzzle. A mathematical puzzle. Out of three and five comes four."

"Oh, all right," Val said slowly. "Yeah, I get it. But even if we figure the math part out, how does that serve us?"

"Look at this indentation on the pedestal," Pip said, pointing at the round hole in the middle of the altar, lower than the rest by maybe an inch. "I think it's like a pressure plate. When the right amount of water is placed on it, the water from the trapdoors will stop filling the chamber, and we're saved."

"Why do I suddenly feel like I'm stuck in a poor *Indiana Jones* parody...?" Val mumbled mostly to himself, scratching his head. Nodding at Pip, he added, "We'll do that, then. All right, so we obviously can't fill the three-gallon jug with four gallons of water."

Pip dared a chuckle and surprised himself at the genuine levity in his voice and the fact that he wasn't as afraid as he'd expected. Pondering on the possibilities behind it, Pip came to the conclusion that while some of that temperance was undoubtedly due to the two men with him, some of it was born of the scholarly knowledge he possessed and had used to untangle their current predicament. That gave him self-confidence and made him smile.

"I already know the answer," he said, having calculated the steps in his head. Proceeding with a practical demonstration, Pip filled the five-gallon jug with water, and then poured three gallons out of it into the three-gallon jug—which he then emptied and refilled with the remaining two gallons in the five-gallon jug. Wagging the jugs in front of Val and Jinn triumphantly, he said, "And now there's room for one more gallon in the three-gallon jug, so if I fill the five-gallon jug and use it to fill the remainder of the three-gallon jug—"

"You get four gallons left in the five gallon jug," Val finished Pip's statement, grinning ear to ear at having figured out the process.

"Right," Pip said. Then he refilled the five-gallon jug, emptying one gallon into the three-gallon jug, and then placing the bigger jug with now four gallons of water onto the indentation on the pedestal.

Nothing happened.

The water level continued to rise.

Until....

The indentation on the pedestal dropped an inch, a low click sounded, echoing deeper undertones within the walls around them, and the little holes near the floor level closed, stopping the increase of water within the closed chamber.

Val was the first to let out a chuckling, breathless sigh, and Pip and Jinn mirrored it a second later. "Amazing, Pip. You saved us." Val's sky-blue eyes raked over Pip's face and torso, and Pip had a feeling that if they'd not been in a locked room up to their thighs in cold water they would've been going at it like rabbits in heat.

Suddenly there was a shrill yelp that didn't sound very far off. A loud *chuck* cut it in half, and Pip shivered in nervousness. "What was that...?"

Jinn sneered, seemingly calloused. "*That* sounded like the Axe of Woe. Our pursuers must've entered the maze from another location than we if they ended in the Hall of Broken Wishes this quickly."

Pip was having a hard time adjusting to the realization that their expedition had been busy exploring this underground urban site for near a year, and all the while they'd been walking on lethal ground. At any time they could've triggered a trap and died where they stood. In a storm of emotions, Pip came to understand just how close he'd come to never getting the chance to tell Val how he felt or be with him at all.

And in all honesty, they still might not. Not with mortal dangers lurking behind every corner and inside every chamber they had yet to see. Taking a deep breath, Pip calmed himself with the knowledge that, whatever happened, he'd remain strong. And if he and Val did indeed survive this ordeal, Pip would make sure they'd not only start a relationship but they'd build a life together—forever.

Then guilt gnawed at his gut. Stealing a glance at Jinn, Pip knew that a good chunk of his heart wanted Jinn too. He'd been perfect from the first apparition to this steadfast and courageous leader who sought only their safety and wished only their protection. And here Pip was thinking only of Val—when his heart was singing a love song for the mighty genie too.

To reconcile these emotions was not feasible at the moment, though, and snapping his attention back to the matter at hand, he asked, "I don't want any axes to fall on us, so where to now? The water stopped rising, but there are still no doors or—"

Right then the floor vanished from beneath their feet.

Falling into the pool of cold water and the deep, dark chasm underneath, all three men were swept away by the powerful swirling vortex sucking them down to unknowable depths until they all drowned in a wave of darkness.

Chapter Eight

COUGHING vehemently, Val awoke.

Spewing out the remnants of cold water from his aching, burning lungs, he pried his eyes open, scanning his surroundings in a daze. Drenched to the bone and with his clothes stuck to his skin uncomfortably tight, Val managed to raise his head enough to see where he was.

The chamber was dank and dark, but a faint glow from luminescent mold on the stone walls gave enough light for him to see Pip lying nearby, motionless, and fear gripped him with sharp nails. *Please, oh, Father Odin, let him be only unconscious, not dead.*

After scrambling to his feet but then falling down on his wobbly knees, Val crawled toward Pip, who suddenly jerked and coughed out water. "Oh, thank the gods...," Val whispered in a wave of relief as he drew the younger man into his lap and gathered him close, surrounding his lankier figure with his own more athletic and wiry body. Gently rocking his lover in his arms, he pressed his damp cheek against the moist head of sandy-blond hair that belonged to the man he wanted more than anything.

"Val—" Pip's voice shattered as the coughs wracked his body.

"It's all right, Pip," he murmured in Pip's ear, sighing, deeply relieved at having Pip back.

Then a new fear took hold of him, and his gaze darted around searching for their colossal genie. When he didn't find him anywhere, his heart stopped beating and his mood sank lower than the underground city they were lost in. "Jinn…?"

"Jinn…?" Pip's shrill, alarmed voice rose to accompany his, and Pip fought with his remaining strength to get up and look for their companion. "Jinn, where are you?"

"We'll find him, Pip," Val reassured him, getting up too, though his feet shook under him, as if unsure whether they could hold his weight. Having been an immortal and a lesser god for what felt like an eternity already, being this helpless and weak was not a comfortable feeling in the slightest. "I promise we will find him. We won't leave him here."

"That's mighty nice and considerate of you, Val. I'm truly honored."

Jinn entered the circle of low glimmering light, brushing his wet jeans with his hands but to no real avail. His long black hair cascaded down in heavy wet strands, and he'd removed his white T-shirt. His powerful chest with its gigantic muscles shimmered, wet and delicious. If their situation had not been so desperate, Val would've jumped the man.

As it was, Pip beat him to it, crying out with glee and pouncing on the genie like an attacking lion cub, with single-minded ferocity and enthusiasm.

"Don't ever scare me like that again!" Pip mumbled against Jinn's massive chest until Jinn took pity on him, grabbed his butt, and hoisted him up so that their faces were level. Pip proceeded to rain kisses all over Jinn, who chuckled in response, holding the young man close and murmuring soothing words and sounds to him.

Pip was not alone in his overwhelming relief—despite the continuous hazardous situation, they were all together again. No obstacle, no puzzle, and no enemy could stop them as long as they had each other's comforting presence.

Without a word, Val joined the group hug, his arms around Pip's and Jinn's backs, his lips searching for a spot on Jinn's face that wasn't being smothered and covered by Pip's ardent advances. Rising up on his toes, Val kissed Jinn's cheek, feeling the smooth, moist skin, the scent of sandalwood and jasmine filling his nose, and when Jinn's lips covered his own, Val knew theirs was an unusual relationship. And then when Pip's lips met theirs in a tentative attempt at a three-way kiss, Val admitted theirs was a ménage of love.

Suddenly the chamber shook and quaked, and a screeching sound emanated from the walls—that were now sliding toward them inch by torturous inch.

"Oh my God...," Pip said, inhaling sharply.

"Incentive," Jinn said calmly, lowering Pip to his feet, looking around as the walls on two sides started closing in on them. "To force us to move before we have a chance to rest or recompose. Come on." Gesturing Val and Pip to follow, Jinn hurried to the other end of the shady room, where a rectangular opening stood. Darkness pulsated behind the opening as if the heart of an invisible beast lay beyond, just waiting for them to enter and be devoured.

It wasn't like they had a choice in the matter, as the walls came ever closer, and soon the doorway would be too narrow to get through. Jinn nodded at Val, who knew to take the lead, as Jinn would assume the rear, both men instinctively keeping Pip between them, out of harm's way.

A whoosh of warm air brushed against Val's face, as real as a touch, and he shivered in his cold, wet clothes. But then he had other things to worry about when, having taken only a meager few steps, the heavily hanging silence was pierced by sharp metallic sounds, like knives sharpened or razor blades clanging.

"What's that...?" Pip's trembling voice came right behind Val, and he felt Pip's hands fisting the back of his cotton dress shirt that was turning rigid as it slowly dried off.

"Oh, no...." Jinn exhaled behind them, and that was not a soothing sound. "The Hall of Earthly Desires." Jinn's voice grew rugged and dangerous. "Listen to me, and for the love of all the gods in the known omniverse, pay attention! Do *not* get distracted. You will see... things. Ignore them, or pay the price. That was my downfall. Let it not be yours." Staring into the dusky void, he added, "Speed and caution are of the essence here. Watch your step, but keep moving."

The warnings rippled ominously through Val, and for a passing breath he longed for his godly days when he had no cause for fear. Now he was not a god, but he wasn't a coward either.

The echoes of metal on metal clashing and grinding grew louder as they seemed to approach them. Or, as Val suspected was more likely, they were walking toward whatever created those vile, chilling sounds.

Something brushed past him so closely that he felt the breeze against his forehead and the scathing touch of something real. Reacting instinctively, he jerked back, shock at unseen terrors reaching out to find him.

"There's something—" he started, baffled.

"Keep moving," Jinn ordered gruffly behind him, and even though Pip stood between them, Val felt the genie's push on his back.

Something whisked past him quickly, the whistle of it passing nearly deafening him. He stopped and tilted his head around to hear better. Great machines stirred in the dark invisibility behind the thick walls, but there was a smaller underlying sound, a sort of muffled click—and something flew past him again. This time Val felt feathers touch the tip of his nose. An animal? A bird?

He had no time for reflection as a series of clicks came from all around, and then there were flying things everywhere. Pain cut through Val's blinded senses when something hit his arm. Just as he fumbled for the object that had pierced his shirt and grazed his flesh until it bled in tiny droplets, and found a sharp dart there, Jinn shouted, "Run, damn you!"

Yanking the dart out of his arm, tearing the shirtsleeve in the process, Val picked up the pace.

And then all hell broke loose.

Darts and arrows shot out of tiny slits on the walls in rapid succession in all directions, high and low alike, and Val grabbed Pip's arms fiercely and sprinted into a run, dodging the flying objects as best he could, and all the while pulling Pip behind him. Apparently there were several rows of arrow slits on the walls, because Val felt darts brush past his head as well as his feet, and the clicking and creaking sounds all around indicated that the metal tips of the arrowheads had hit something other than flesh, and the wooden arrow shafts had broken or fallen to the floor.

But then a new sound emerged amidst the whooshes, pops, and clicks. A low buzzing pitch began to rise steadily, until Val felt chills crawl on his skin and shoot down his spine. And the projectiles kept on coming.

Suddenly something glinted bright in the darkness, right in front of his face. Val nearly tripped over himself, backpedaling from the huge blade that had shot out of the wall not two inches from his nose. "Holy shit!" His balance was off, and he fell backward—over Pip, who hit Val's back running with an audible *"oomph!"* as his forward momentum was abruptly halted, which had him staggering back onto Jinn's muscular chest.

Luckily for all of them, Jinn was on top of things, as usual. Growling, he picked Pip up by the waist under his left arm and Val under his right arm, and dashed into high speed like his life depended on it. And dangling helplessly against Jinn's sturdy side, hanging on for dear life, Val couldn't get past the idea that it just might. The soles of Jinn's feet scraped the floor made of hewn stone blocks, but the only sparks that flew came from the shower of blades, circular saws, and other shiny, sharp stabbing weapons attempting to cut off their path—and cut them in pieces. They shot out of the walls, the metallic clinks deafening, and the buzz of swirling blades sounded like an angry swarm of killer bees—made of razor blades.

Even though Val was in effect being carried, or dragged, along the horrible corridor of deathly weapons flying and piercing the air, he was panting, as if he were the one doing the running. "J-Jinn...," he mumbled, trying to get this detestable carnival ride to end, nausea churning his stomach into swelling riptides and filling his mouth with bitter acids.

When he saw the glitter of ancient gold and silver coins in huge piles and neat stacks all around, Val was certain the weirdness of the situation, the rush of adrenaline, and being hauled around by a colossal genie had made him hallucinate. His hazy sight, just like topside in the desert on extremely hot days when the air rippled with heat waves, seemed to confirm his hypothesis.

But Pip's vibrating, jumping voice brought him down to earth, so to speak. "Val, look. Gold, everywhere. What a find."

The oddest thing, however, was the fact that Jinn cut in—and he wasn't even out of breath from lugging two grown men around, running like Speedy Gonzales, and twisting and turning to avoid the flying deadly contraptions the air was thick with. "They're mirages. Hallucinations of pleasures and gain. I warned you to expect them."

Val felt bile gathering in his mouth, and he coughed at the sour taste, praying to his family of gods to end this suffering sooner rather than later. "By all the gods, Jinn, stop...."

The mumbled words had barely left his lips when Jinn slowed down enough to let Val and Pip get back on their feet, both craving Jinn's support in their unsteadiness, both holding their bellies and covering their mouths. "Are you two quite undamaged? Are you hurt?"

Val waved a trembling hand in denial. "Just sick to my stomach.... Oh, shit, I'm going to hurl."

"Not before me...," Pip squeaked, spinning around, dropping to his knees, and holding on to his stomach, though from the lack of retching sounds and smell of vomit he successfully repressed the sickly spell.

Having sat down flat on his ass, Val too was beginning to get his bearings back, as the dizzy swaying motion that had caused the nauseating sensations was over. "Holy hell... that was some ride."

Jinn smirked. "Now thank your chosen deities for me carrying you out of harm's way. If I had not, you'd still be there, chasing after riches, wealth, and material possessions—and, if you were lucky, grasping only air, but in the most likely scenario you'd have ended up with a number of puncture wounds. And years from now, when another expedition would come along, they'd find your dried-up corpse hanging from a blade sticking out of the wall and congratulate themselves for not being on your end of the stick." He shook his head wearily. "The Hall of Earthly Desires is not a place for greedy or ambitious or horny people to have any hope of surviving."

"You didn't know the puzzle in the water chamber, but you did know the deadly obstacles we'd face back there," Pip commented from the floor, gazing up so high to reach Jinn's eyes that his craning neck must've jammed up. "That was your crime, wasn't it? Greed for earthly delights."

Sighing ruefully, Jinn finally nodded. "Genies who were obsessed with material gain or earthly pleasures beyond all reason were bound in punishment to material objects and wishes of mortals over their own. The oil lamp I'm bound to is a symbol of the very reasons for my incarceration. The fire within the lamp burns, just as all the fleeting, casual sex I had back then burned me to cinders, and incinerated my moral backbone and my adherence to the rules that the society was built upon."

"Your crime was *sex*?" Pip's tone was incredulous and dismayed at once. "The wrong kind of sex? Too much sex?"

Jinn chuckled, but Val could tell there was precious little humor there to back it up. "No and no. Not wrong or too much. Just… with the wrong person."

"Oh-oh…," Pip huffed, in anticipation of the revelation.

"I seduced… the prince of our people… during his wedding banquet…. That didn't sit too well with the genie elders, as I'm sure you can imagine." For the first time ever, Val saw Jinn's face redden, but he suspected this wasn't a treasured memory of arousal and sexual conquest but embarrassment over… well, Val wasn't sure what, exactly. But whatever the cause of that shame, it most certainly wasn't positive pride over his accomplishment.

"Oh, Jinn, I'm sorry," Pip said, climbing to his feet and slipping his small hand to hold Jinn's bigger hand.

"No, don't be," Jinn stated emphatically, but keeping his tone soft. "I behaved badly because I wanted him—not to love and keep, but to conquer and fuck. It was right for me to receive punishment."

"A pretty harsh punishment for such a small infraction," Pip remarked, his frown and pout telltale signs of his opinion. "Especially since there were two of you in that bed. I mean, I assume it was a bed...." Pip's voice trailed off for a second before he shook his head in frustration. "You didn't force him, did you?"

Now it was Jinn's turn to furrow his brow. "No. He came willingly. And yes, it was in a bed. At first, at least...." This time his sheepish blush was less embarrassed, Val noted, amused, and he couldn't keep the grin off his own face.

But Val had other concerns that made his smile vanish into thin air. "Speaking of the lamp... where is it? If it's still topside, those guys will, if they haven't already, probably ransack the campsite upside down looking for it."

Pip smiled reassuringly. "Don't worry, Val. I have it with me."

Confused, Val doubted his eyesight in the dwindling darkness for a second—before coming to the conclusion that Pip must've been wrong. There was no room on his person, or Jinn's, for that matter, to hide a sizable lump like the oil lamp. "Where?"

Chuckling low and meekly, Pip said, "I used up a wish to reduce its size to something more manageable so I could hide it better. I have it on my key chain."

"Your...." Val just couldn't find adequate words to describe how stupefied he felt. He knew Pip could be resourceful in the extreme, but for him to have foreseen this kind of scenario beforehand was a testament to his smarts. And that just made Val fall madly and hopelessly in love with Pip all over again. "All right, then." Taking a good long look around, Val commented, "I take it we are not yet out of the woods?"

"No," Jinn confirmed with a curt nod. "There are about half a dozen challenges before the game is over. I do realize this is not a game, so let's keep moving. The walls came at us last time, so this time I suspect spikes from the floor or the ceiling as we get crushed or run through."

"Charming," Val mumbled, stepping close to Pip and taking his hand. "Let's go, then."

Once again Jinn took the lead, and they progressed toward the end of the hall. The noise born of the fast-spinning circular saws and rapidly stabbing blades had ceased, but now the silence pressed down on them, heavy and thick with promises of further ominous dangers. The narrow corridor kept winding and twisting and kept them guessing what would face them around every corner. But despite a few cobwebs sans spiders, gritty sand and pebbles beneath the soles of their feet, and dust cascading over them in slow-motion featherlight clouds, nothing and no one met them in either friendship or hostility.

When the light began to increase again, they knew to expect the worst.

The huge chamber that opened up before them was naturally cavernous with rough-hewn walls, but with jewels embedded in the walls and ceiling, and an eerie glow emanated from their depths. The floor, however, was covered with blue glazed tiles and adorned with gilded carvings of unknown wavy writing. A feeling of vast space surrounded Val, and he tugged Pip closer to him, placing his arm on his shoulder to keep him near.

"Oh, Val, look," Pip cried out keenly, pointing at the center of the chamber. The base of a tall pedestal stood there, and upon it were two stone statues frozen in a fighting stance, appearing as a unified shape of clashing mythological characters.

Pip longed to see it closer, and he almost did so, but Val tightened his grip, determined not to let the young man out of his sight or out of range of his touch even for a second. "Not a chance, Pip. We can inspect it just fine from here."

Pip gave him a reproachful glare—but then seemed to remember where they were and looked sheepish, whispering apologetic words. Val dared a light chuckle even at the risk of angering whatever gods held this place as their private domain. Hesitant, he closed the distance between them and the two-figured statue cautiously.

"A winged lion and a man-faced bull," Pip observed, his voice echoing hauntingly all over the large chamber. But only Val seemed to notice, while Pip just continued to be mesmerized by the ancient art, his tone steady in its one-track setting. "There's something like this in Persepolis. The bull represents earth and the lion the sun. Well, they would without the wings and the human face." Pip leaned in different directions to assess the statue from various angles. "I've seen this fighting depiction between the bull and the lion before, but not with wings and human faces. Lion statues typically flanked ceremonial doorways and important routes, like in Philae. But this is different."

"Yes," Val agreed, inspecting what he saw with a professional, discerning eye. "That precious blue stone on the floor reminds me of the Ishtar Gate. Lapis lazuli, I think. Persian cultural references abound." Val turned to Jinn, who stood behind them watching the statue with wary eyes. "Is your genie culture based on the Persian culture, or vice versa?"

Jinn's electric-blue eyes flashed. "Ask them yourself."

Both Val and Pip stared at Jinn dumbfounded, as if he'd spoken a foreign language.

"But be forewarned, only one of them tells the truth," Jinn added, as if the clarification was lucid and enlightening instead of insanely confusing. Pip opened and closed his mouth like a fish caught on dry land, and Val felt a similar desperate bewilderment of being yanked out of the familiar into this strangeness. Apparently Jinn decided to take pity on them, because with a warning tone he added only, "They're magical. They're golems."

Startled, Val stepped further away from the statue and towed Pip frantically with him, and then placed the smaller man behind his own back to shield him from whatever was to come. Fortunately, they didn't have to wait for long.

The bull with a man's bearded face turned in their direction.

The magical substance it was made of, reminiscent of stone, rippled like water, adjusting to the new position before solidifying again. Only dead gray stone eyes stared back at Val, but he felt there was a presence in there. A kind of life force, and this alien being made Val want to do what Jinn had done and grab Pip and run like hell.

Then the lion shifted as well, facing them stoically. The yellow stone gave the lion's features and fur a golden glow, and the stone's veins created a shimmering, lifelike effect that was very unsettling for Val.

Yes, in his time and form as both god and man Val had seen much, heard of more, experienced plenty, and knew that the Veil had hidden many things from the eyes of the mundane mortal world. But at this specific moment in time and space, Val was one of two guardians of Pip's life, in addition to Jinn, and he cursed the past relinquishment of his divine powers. Those sure could've come in handy right about now.

"You can only speak to one of them, and even then only once," Jinn said behind them, his tone grim. "One tells the truth, the other lies. So make your question matter."

"Surely you've done this bit before?" Val asked him anxiously, waiting for something between an explanation and an escape plan. "Don't you know the correct answer, or the right question, or the solution to this riddle?"

Jinn shook his head, his expression grave. "This is the Hall of the Dying Breath. I've heard of this place, but I've never been here. I fell in the previous chamber in my time. I do not have the answer you seek."

"I know this," Pip murmured quietly, carefully inspecting the two unmoving shapes of stone that held vitality beyond a mortal's understanding. Val was worried Pip would take too much of this upon himself, and pulled him against him, back to chest. He felt Pip's rapid heartbeat and swift breaths as vibrations against his skin, and he wrapped his arms around Pip protectively and possessively. "This is Knights and Knaves. It's a logic puzzle. There's supposed to be a right question that makes it irrelevant whether or not the speaker tells the truth or lies. One can deduce the answer logically, if I remember correctly."

"If you say so," Val said, suppressing his disbelief, because if Pip believed he could do it then Val's ridiculous concerns would only exacerbate the situation. And they did need an answer.

And soon, too, before this place began to spew out motivational, deadly tools to test their resolve under dangerous conditions, their ability to think on their feet, and their problem-solving capability with distractions all around. And Val had not yet gotten his chance to be with Pip, so he wasn't prepared to go through death's door at this juncture. He'd have Pip's heart and body for his own first—no matter what.

"Choose what you say or ask carefully," Jinn noted, standing next to Val like the rock of the world, protective with his mere serene presence. "Because, of those two doors leading out of this chamber, only one leads to safety, life, happiness, all that and more. The other... you don't want to know where it takes you, and I'd rather not find out either, if you get my drift."

Only then did Val notice the two big oval doorways on opposite sides of the chamber, as they lay hidden in the dark shadows with an ominous feel attached to them, like an invisible monster breathing hotly against his face. Neither doorway felt more appealing than the other, and Val definitely didn't need to hear any details about what variety of horrors lay in wait behind the wrong door and what these imaginary beasts had in store for them.

Whatever the gruesome scenario, it seemed each statue was a guardian to an equivalent doorway.

"All right, then," Val said, pulling himself back from the brink of anxiety to look at Pip with anticipation of release from this unease as soon as the riddle was solved and they could take the exit from the magical labyrinth, hoping it was clearly marked with huge blinking red block letters, like regular exits. "So, Pip, what's the question?"

Suddenly Pip blushed deeply, and as endearing as it was to Val, he had a bad feeling he wasn't going to like his answer. "Um… I can't remember, sorry." Val's shoulders slumped, and his expression must have betrayed his disappointment, but upon seeing the sadness in Pip's hazel eyes, he regretted his reaction immediately. "Knights and Knaves was one of those irritating riddles I could never figure out so I… forgot…. I'm sorry."

Looking despondent didn't suit Pip, and Val pulled the guy back into his arms, stroking his sandy-blond hair gently. "No, I'm sorry, baby. You've done so much for us already, Pip. Now it's our turn." Without letting go of Pip, whose arms had wound around his waist, seemingly pleased with Val's choice of endearment, Val turned to face Jinn, who stood in place like a stone statue of a god of masculinity. "Jinn, any suggestions? Bright insights? Inspired epiphanies?"

Jinn shrugged a little, as if impassive, but Val knew the man cared for Pip more than he let on, so he'd do anything to get Pip out safely—and indirectly all of them too. "It seems unlikely that if we ask only one of them which door to choose we'll get a clear answer or be any closer to determining which one speaks the truth and—"

"That's it!" Val shouted, releasing Pip to walk closer to the statues, watching them intently. A sudden revelation had come over him, and he understood how this puzzle worked. "Jinn, you're a genius!"

"I am?" Jinn remarked, curious and bewildered, but then his facial expression shifted to beaming. "Yes, I *am*." He made a pleased chuckle, his electric-blue eyes raking over Val's drenched body. Despite the doubt that he looked good enough to be devoured with eyes, he couldn't deny the flush of heat that the intense gaze created within him. He might have been in love with Pip, but Jinn spoke to a part of him he didn't want to bury under hesitation and convention forever. His new mortal existence was too short to not live life to the fullest extent.

But unfortunately for his needy body, now was not the time to act on those feelings. Still, from the way a knowing grin graced Jinn's luscious lips, Val got the sense that the genie knew exactly what was going through his mind. To his surprise, he didn't mind, even if Jinn did.

Checking the statues with a cautious yet discerning eye, he said, "I think we should ask one of them about the other—"

Pip's amused laugh cut him abruptly short. "Come on, Val. I know you're pretty darn good with your deductive reasoning skills, but we're pressed for time here and this isn't a lecture hall. We don't require explanations, or at least they can wait. Just ask your question."

Nervousness hit Val like a sledgehammer. "But… what if I'm wrong about—"

Pip shushed him. "Don't start second-guessing yourself now. You can do this. I know it. I have faith in you, Val." Pip's sweet, kind, and loving gaze landed on both men, and Val's heart jumped. "I believe in you both." While Jinn had the appearance of the proverbial cat that ate the canary, glowing in the warm light of Pip's appreciation, Val was busy trying to rein in his flustered state—and failing. Oh, how that young man spoke to his heart….

With his newfound self-confidence, as rediscovered by Pip, Val turned to the statues that stood so still that if he hadn't previously seen them move, he would not have believed them to be golems capable of mimicking life and movement. Seeing a winged lion speak was not on his list of things to see in his lifetime, as fascinating as that would have been, so Val spoke to the man-faced bull standing up on his hind legs while his front hooves were in an attacking pose against the chest of the winged lion, which held a similar stance with his paws up and his feathered wings spread wide for balance.

"Would the lion tell me that the door he guards leads to safety?" Yes, he heard the uncertainty in his own voice even though he believed he had deduced and phrased the question correctly. Nonetheless, his tone cracked hopelessly at the end. Val could feel the tension in Jinn and Pip, and heard them draw in a breath and hold it.

An eerie quietness evoked all kinds of hellish images in Val's overactive imagination.

The bull with the human male face turned back toward the lion, who did the same, so they assumed their original positions. "No."

Clear-cut answer, Val thought, and felt a chill at the emotionally cold voice, devoid of all aspects of humanity. *All right,* he said to himself, *onward to the conclusion.*

"Which door is it, then?" Pip's small voice inquired.

"The lion's door."

Pip frowned, but as far as Val could tell not from disbelief or doubt per se, but from the barely concealed eagerness to hear how Val had come to that conclusion. But before Pip spoke at all, he suddenly wrinkled his nose in distaste. "Do you smell that?"

Pip was right, as usual. A faint hissing sound accompanied an unpleasant, stinging odor that pierced the air, filling Val's lungs until his tongue was covered in a tangy taste that nauseated him and was associated in his mind with poisonous ingredients of nature and the animal kingdom. A strong sensation of suffocation began to creep into his consciousness, but it took him a moment to process it.

His eyes flew wide as the realization hit him dead-on. "*Gas!*"

Grabbing Pip's and Jinn's arms, Val sprang into motion, running toward the oval opening on the lion's side of the chamber. The room swirled around him, and the air rippled in waves of dizzying, noxious fumes as he hurried toward the door. Before he could even touch it, the stone slab protecting it slid aside, and they dashed into the pitch-black corridor, almost tumbling over each other in their haste. They took several tremulous steps to distance themselves from the chamber that had filled with invisible, breathable death.

Coughing, Val finally stopped his hasty progress and crouched a bit to catch his breath as he heard the stone door close behind them and fresh air surrounded him again. Inhaling deeply, Val was certain he'd never before considered oxygen such a sweet fragrance as he did right at that moment.

He slid down to sit on the ground, his back against the rough-hewn stone wall, letting himself relax just a bit. He heard more than saw in the darkness when Pip and Jinn joined him on the floor.

"Dying breath indeed…," Val mumbled sardonically.

"Well, that was a pip experience…." Pip's words inspired chuckles all around. Pip's hand found Val's, and he squeezed back with happy relief. "How did you figure out the riddle?" Yes, Val's little scientist and his enthusiastic mind were obviously hard at work on recent events, and Val didn't ever want to squash that endearing quality.

Coughing the last remnants of his oxygen-deprived state, Val glanced at Pip and Jinn to see if he had their undivided attention, seeing their shadowy shapes in the bleak dark and the dim glow of their eyes, and felt nervous when he found them both listening intently and hanging on his every word. "Long story short, it didn't matter which one of the statues I asked about which door, or who told the truth and who lied. What did matter was including both guardians in the question. Because only then would a *yes* mean that the door in question led to peril, and a *no* meant that that particular door was the safe route out." The baffled looks Pip and Jinn exchanged suggested that they didn't follow Val's train of thought.

"Now you're just showing off," Pip giggled, breathless, still coughing every now and then. "I don't get it."

"Me neither," Jinn commented from the floor on the opposite side of the corridor, his feet tangling with Val's as they both stretched out, and it was the most comfortable and homey feeling he'd shared with the powerful genie. Jinn's reassuring presence made butterflies dance around in Val's belly, and the cozy reaction warmed his heart like no other. The warmth and heat didn't take anything away from his feelings for Pip but instead complemented them until they all rolled into one big bundle of emotions.

"If the bull was telling the truth and the lion would've answered *no*, then the lion's answer would've been a lie, which translates to the fact the door he guards does in fact lead to safety." Val checked the expressions of both men and found them leaning toward him and concentrating. "If the bull was lying, then the lion would've answered truthfully with his *yes*, and again the door in question would lead to safety. So, you see it didn't matter who spoke the truth or which door I inquired about. And if the answer would've been *yes*, the reverse would've come into effect, and the door would've led to our demise." Confused smiles greeted him, and he asked playfully, "Should I explain it again?"

Laughs and waves of hand stopped him, and Val felt better about their entrapment in this dismal maze of deadly traps and lethal enemies. Yes, they'd be all right.

In a blink of an eye, distant echoes of screams riddled the air, followed by sharp *tchak* sounds, one right after another in a rapid series, and then only silence. Val shivered. Apparently their enemies were having rotten luck with their advance through the maze, but considering they were after Jinn's omnipotent genie powers and his and Pip's deaths, Val didn't shed a single tear for their faceless mercenary foes.

"Ouch...," Jinn commented, with a hint of a sympathetic look. "That sounded like the Pit of Despair. Big drop, sharp spikes. Bad for them." Glancing at Val with a wicked grin, Jinn added, "Good for us. Less of them to pursue and kill us, right?"

"Gloating doesn't become anyone," Pip murmured disapprovingly, and then he got up, leaning against the wall for support for a second. "It's unethical—and most unattractive to boot." Throwing a meaningful glare at both men, Pip continued down the corridor away from the statue chamber of gaseous death. Quickly, Val and Jinn scrambled up on their feet, mildly embarrassed, and hurried to catch up with the young man. It made sense to pick up the pace since there was no telling what motivation-inducing machinations awaited them next in the darkness.

Fortunately, they didn't have to wait long at all before a dim circle of light pierced the gloom of the corridor, and a new chamber opened in front of them. Before they could form any kind of opinion of their surroundings, blinding heat blasted against their faces like waves of smoldering caresses. Smothering smoke clouds from lava pools and gas fires filled the cavernous chamber so it was hard to see anything specific, and the smell of smoke attacked them something fierce.

"Oh...," Jinn sighed longingly, and his expression matched the blissful utterance. "The Halls of the Fires of Creation... my old stomping grounds. Ah, so good to be home."

"Right... well, I love what you've done with the place," Val managed to say, not sure if he was being meanly sarcastic or sincerely complimentary. But Jinn's grin told Val he knew exactly what Val had meant, and Val had his answer then, when the sweetness of that smile made his heart flutter. "If you've been here before, you must know what to expect. Another puzzle? Shifting walls? Fire-breathing monsters?" he asked even as the three of them ventured deeper into the smoky unknown of the cavern, and their wet yet stiff clothes began to steam and dry slowly in the heat of the chamber.

Jinn chuckled. "Mostly the latter. Usually there is a physical confrontation of sorts." The answer didn't stop their progress, but it did make their movements wary and cautious.

"So, there must be something to the myth about genies as creatures of fire, yes?" Val wasn't sure if he wanted to know or not. The scientist within Val always sought more questions to ask while the child within longed to learn everything in the world. Whether answers were forthcoming or not, a part of Val would end up satisfied—and a part disappointed.

"Now, Val," Pip scolded at his side. "Don't pry. I'm sure Jinn will tell us all about himself when he so chooses." And then Pip did the most amazing thing Val had ever seen him do. He took Val's hand in his own, and then Jinn's hand in the other, and interlaced their fingers. Val had never felt so connected with Pip, not even when they'd been kissing in Pip's tent. Turning to face Jinn, Val observed Jinn giving him the come-hither lift of his chin, with a wicked smile, and without hesitation, Val extended his hand and took Jinn's hand in his own. Forming a peculiar love triangle with Pip and Jinn, all of them lost in an abandoned maze in an ancient, ruined underground city, Val felt happier than he'd ever felt. This was how he wanted things to be. Just the three of them against the world, side by side, loving and being loved by each other.

But perhaps a happy ending wasn't in the cards for them.

A sharp popping noise deafened Val in a blink of an eye, and right after that blink, he was no longer holding Pip's hand.

It was as if Pip had been torn away from Val's grasp. Crashing to the ground, Pip fell backward hard, as if he'd been pushed from the front, and then he collapsed on the cavern floor like a limp ragdoll.

And then Val saw it.

A red smudge on Pip's chest, just below the collarbone, close to the heart.

And the stain grew darker and larger with every heartbeat Val missed as shock turned him into a statue, unable to move, to blink, to breathe—only able to stare, horrified, as life left Pip's body. His chest stopped rising, his parted lips let out a last gasp, his hazel eyes fluttered and closed, his lovely face grew blank, and all discernible signs of life abandoned him.

No, no, no…. Val's mind turned inside out and flipped off the lights as the mortal man he was within died with Pip in an underground cavern filled with smoke, heat, and fires. For Val, with Pip gone, the very light of life faded away, and only cold and bleak darkness would be his future from now on into infinity.

Chapter Nine

DURING his long life, Jinn had experienced loss many times over.

But this….

Right before Jinn's eyes, Pip's heart stopped beating, and Val's defeated essence felt just as dead to Jinn, who watched Pip's lifeless body lie on the gray stone floor of the cavern, surrounded by fires, but his body slowly losing its inherent warmth.

My beloved wish master is gone.

He lifted his gaze to a distraught Val, who stood in place, frozen, unmoving. Shock, nausea, terror, pain—all those were present on Val's handsome Viking god's face, like he was nothing without Pip. And that Jinn understood down in the very marrow of his bones.

Unable to look at Val's expression of utter misery and hopelessness, Jinn turned in the direction the deadly shot had come from. His ears were still ringing from the strange sound, unlike any he'd ever heard before.

He could see a man there, by the entrance into the chamber where they'd been before they'd bravely entered to find whatever was in here waiting for them. Who knew the enemy would strike at them from behind?

Dressed in black and what looked like armor plating, only softer and thinner, the man lifted his hand and aimed a piece of metal at Jinn. It didn't take a genius to figure out that it was a weapon, but Jinn made no attempt to move away. As a genie, his powers of self-preservation would stop whatever force that new weapon expelled.

But then the man stepped forward, with a triumphant, gloating smugness on his face—and there was a click right beneath his feet.

Surprised, the man looked down, at first not realizing or caring that he'd set off a trap, just noting an innocuous sound that had risen from underneath him.

Before he could wrap his brain around that fact, it was already far too late.

Monstrous fireballs emanating heat and roaring flames shot out from the walls from six different directions, all converging on the man's position. Jinn saw his eyes widen and heard him gasp, and then the fireballs hit him in a flash of blinding light and thundering sound, blasting the guy to smithereens in a blink of an eye. Jinn watched it happen and felt nothing but revenge fulfilled—and then sorrow and emptiness.

Except... there was a way out of this misery.

Grabbing Val's arm but getting no response from the man, he spoke in earnest, keeping his tone as coherent, clear, and steady as he could. "Val, make a wish." He squeezed Val's arm tighter, and, blinking, Val finally turned to him, his handsome face covered in streaks of tears, his expression confused, as if he didn't understand what was going on. Knowing this underwater feeling all too well, Jinn gathered all his inner fortitude as he said again, "Val, take Pip's key chain. The lamp is on it. Rub it, make a wish, and I can destroy those men who did this. I cannot follow a new wish master until all three wishes have been fulfilled—or until the wish master dies. I still cannot use my powers to get us out of here, but you are able to use it now for *this* purpose. Do it." Jinn felt safe suggesting this to

Val, who understood the nature of the world. Pip, on the other hand, was too good a person to ever consider destroying other people just to save himself, which is why Jinn had not proposed this option to Pip.

Pushing Val to the ground less than subtly had the desired effect, and Val's trembling hands fumbled with Pip's khaki pants pockets until he came up with Pip's key chain, that had several keys, a flash drive, and a heart-shaped amber jewel decoration on it—and the miniaturized magical oil lamp.

"Got it," Val said in a hushed tone, and Jinn could see how he fought the urge to look at Pip and stayed focused on the key chain. His fingers wet with tears, Val rubbed the side of the electric blue, gold-trimmed oil lamp, and Jinn felt the pulse of fire pass through him, giving him the usual rush of sensual delight at the prospect of a new wish master. It was the only positive aspect of being incarcerated in a magical lamp. Looking up at Jinn with teary eyes that began to burn with fury and revenge, Val growled, "Get them, Jinn. All those men. Take them out—by any means necessary."

The fire of a genie kindled within Jinn, and he felt the wave of the omnipotent powers wash over him, through him, imbuing him with magical potency beyond the comprehension of mere mortal men. "As you wish, master."

HAUNTED and justifiably infuriated by the desperate sorrow enveloping Val in its cold-as-death shroud, Jinn gathered all the immense powers of a genie around him, like a tornado sucking up air into a whirlwind. It was, for all intents and purposes, an act of god—or a godlike being.

Unleashed, Jinn let his gaze pierce the surrounding walls, both natural and constructed alike. Val's wish had given him the power to search and destroy all their enemies, and as if the separating stone enclosures had magically turned transparent, Jinn could see them all wherever they were in the labyrinth, the city, or the site above ground.

There were nine of them, divided in four distinct locations.

Two were the closest, advancing on Jinn's position. But his own position was far from precarious as he watched through the clear walls that to them appeared as solid walls with nothing visible beyond.

Letting out a low growl, Jinn teleported through the air in a whoosh of air, carried by the force of the wish as easily as wind lifted wings of birds and butterflies. While he moved through a rift in time-space, Jinn's snap of fingers brought all nine men to a single location, which in this case he chose to be the Hall of Animate Retribution, a large cavern where there was seemingly no way out. Jinn knew the place well and anticipated the fate the men would confront and endure there. But he still had his own score to settle first.

The Hall of Animate Retribution opened up before him, vast and silent. No sounds apart from the alarmed voices of the men trapped there could be heard anywhere. The walls were lined with pillar-framed niches of stone statues of ancient warriors, gods of war, and genies hell-bent on revenge. The empty hall had no doors, only a single trapdoor on the ceiling through which most people entered—with no other visible means of escape. Now these men had no way of knowing how they'd appeared from their separate locations around the labyrinth, and thus felt only fear of the unknown.

But Jinn was about to show them something real and tangible to fear.

In a flash of electric-blue light, like a lightning strike, he appeared before them.

All of them—except one—started, raised their automatic weapons, and started blasting toward him, screaming out all their raging emotions. An invisible shield composed of whirling wind and electric shocks rose in front of him as he sauntered toward them, featherlight on his feet. The thundering roar of the weapons made no difference to him, and the bullets whisked away from him, hitting with thuds on the walls around him.

Busy reloading, the mercenaries had fear in their eyes now.

Then that fear mixed with a different kind of concern—terror of the unknown—as Jinn snapped his fingers. And the guns in the hands of these men transformed into… licorice. The long barrels of the automatic weapons bent down, like something edible melting in the sun, and the baffled men quickly discarded them in favor of their other pieces, which were handguns from shoulder and ankle holsters.

Jinn again snapped his fingers. Disgusted *eww* sounds accompanied the shaking of their hands as they tried to get rid of the melting licorice that the guns had magically morphed into. Now mostly without armaments or means of self-defense, the men stared at him, dread and fury in eyes that at that moment lacked professionalism.

Into the loaded silence, Jinn spoke steadfastly, with a warning not even a deaf person could mishear. "This is my home. Around here, people show respect when coming in uninvited to a genie's castle. You are small-minded, loathsome thugs, so prepare to draw in your last breath." Taking in a deep breath, Jinn began to swirl air around him, accumulating a fast gyrating column of air, twisting and rolling until it was only a blur of rushing winds, howling and screaming, hot and cold alike. "I'm going to huff and puff and blow you away. Be glad I'm not a horny little devil but a genie wronged."

The condensed pillar of whirlwind blew out in all directions like a shock wave, and the mercenaries lost their footing as they fell back or were thrown back by the force of pushing air, and they continued to roll backward on the stone floor, hitting the walls heavily, unable to get back up on their feet. Confused with regard to time and place, blinded, they were weakened by the elements of nature surrounding them by the sheer force of a genie's magic.

Allowing the cyclone winds to dissipate, Jinn watched the men shake their heads to try and come around, attempting to scramble back up on their feet, most of them standing in place on shaky legs, disoriented and weary from fighting invisible forces of nature. As a result, they regained their former selves in individual order, advancing on Jinn one after another, which gave him the opportunity to deal with them individually.

Grinning, he said, "You're too dirty." He pointed at the first man, and rapid waters awash with white crests hit him dead-on, and he slammed against the back wall, sputtering and groaning in pain until he fell down, unconscious.

Turning to the second man, Jinn said, "You're too clean." A cloud of dirt and dust surrounded the man, making him choke and cough, and soon he was covered in grime and muck from head to toe. Staggering backward, he tried to get away but without success, so he turned around in blind panic and ran—but his surroundings were too obscured for him to see the wall, so he ran into it full force. With a heavy thud he went down, also very much out of the game.

A third man got up, and having witnessed what Jinn had done to the other two men, hesitated—and brought about his own downfall. "You're too still. Dance for me." A snap of fingers, and the man's feet did move then—without his consent or control— following a rhythm of music inaudible to all. Even to Jinn. But that didn't stop him from having the man magically perform for his pleasure as he kept swaying this way and that, yelping as his feet took him wherever they wanted to go—with his head being none the wiser.

Even though he was enjoying the show, Jinn did not miss another man sprinting toward him in an effort to catch him off guard. The attempt failed miserably as Jinn snapped his fingers and said, "You're too mobile. Freeze!" Before the words had even left his lips, the man stopped his rush of an advance as though his feet were caught in mud. The ice darted up in shiny white needles from the floor, covering his feet and then rising steadily as the air grew colder, and Jinn could see his breaths in puffy clouds of exhales. Frosty sheen blanketed him, and the fear there in his eyes was drawn out—and yet it gave Jinn little satisfaction. He'd always been a lover, not a fighter, and causing harm and misery was not his favorite game.

But this was not a game. This was real and serious, greedy killers seeking ways to use Jinn's unique abilities for their own selfish gain. And there was already a fatality.

No mercy, his thirst for vengeance cried out—even as his conscience knew better and would not allow him to mortally harm these foolish men.

And… his inner genie, the childlike one that allowed nothing serious to touch him, wanted to play.

Four down. Five to go.

The remaining four standing all approached his position at once. Laughing, Jinn pointed at them. "Look at you. Foolish mortals." He pointed at one, snapping his fingers. "Too manly." And the man's militaristic clothing changed in a heartbeat into a long flowing dress of silk and jewelry, and since he'd been running forward, he tripped over the long hem, and down he went.

Moving to the next, Jinn said amusedly, snapping his fingers, "Too girly." The man stopped dead in his tracks in sudden dread, but he didn't have the chance to back off or attack when he suddenly blinked hard. Then his gaze veered off to his comrade trying to get out of the woman's dress he was wearing, but since it was on him by magic it was a hopeless battle.

But this man, however, looked at his colleague with something like lust—and with a winning thrill of the chase gleaming in his eyes, he scampered toward his friend. The man in the dress had managed to get up—only to detect his friend running toward him with a boner. Tugging up the hem of the dress in his hands, he ran the other way, shouting in part frustrated annoyance, part genuine panic. Well, Jinn surmised, that man was not gay.

Turning to the last two men still left standing, Jinn grinned as the men scowled. "Too angry." A snap, and the closer man burst into laughter. Holding his stomach, which soon would begin to ache like a son of a bitch, he kept on cackling like a mad hyena, unable to stop himself or to prevent the act in any way. His face reddened as if he couldn't breathe properly through the hysterical fit, and he fell on the ground on his knees, guffawing insanely.

Jinn faced the last man, who looked around in desperation, realizing he was all alone, unprotected and unarmed. He swallowed and finally looked at Jinn, wide-eyed. Clearly a threat like a full-powered genie had not been mentioned in the job description.

Jinn almost felt sorry for him. Then he remembered Pip lying dead on the rocky floor of a cavern, and his empathy disappeared. "Where is your leader? Which one of these men is he?"

Before he even finished speaking, the man was already pointing to the other side of the chamber. "He's the one lying on the floor. He fell into a room, and there was something there, and it spat on him. He couldn't move. And we couldn't get to him. And then we were already here."

Of the nine men who had entered this cavernous chamber, only one had not moved the entire time, and now Jinn knew why.

But all in good time. Facing the last man on his feet again, he said only, "You're far too happy to be alive when my friend, my wish master, and my love is dead. Lament for him. Like you mean it."

With one last snap of his fingers, Jinn stood in place, watching as the man's eyes began to water and swell. Soon streaks of tears were running down his cheeks like there was no tomorrow. Backing away from Jinn in fear, as he still had control of his feet, he ran off as fast as he could, and Jinn let him.

There was only the one man left, and he wasn't going anywhere.

But topside there were still hostages waiting to be rescued. It wasn't until this very moment when Val had wished him to take out the bad guys that he could utilize his powers to their full effect—though he was still unable to use his might to rescue Pip and Val from the labyrinth itself. He surmised now, in grim hindsight, that he could have asked Pip to wish for this earlier, but Jinn knew he had been selfish. Jinn had longed for more excitement and time with these two men who spoke to his heart—and now he had paid the price for his greed of pleasure, yet again. Pip was dead and Val was broken. The fury within Jinn—for the evil men as well as for his own misdeed—gave him the force and the need to set about his task with a vengeance.

In a flash, Jinn shifted from one place to the next, invisible as all unbound genies had been before the Unveiling, and could still do so for their own safety and survival. Now the white dining tent stood in front of him, the plastic covers and the door flaps fluttering in the rough, dry wind blowing in from the desert. Not even the tents situated close to each other could stop the prevailing harsh climate from reaching him.

Without waiting for anyone to come—not that they could detect him if they did—Jinn entered the tent. The long wooden tables had been cleared and placed at the sides of the tent so that the group of bound people, numbering three dozen in all, sat huddled together in the middle, all looking miserable and weary.

Two men were in the tent with these people. The strange weapons they were carrying, like the ones Jinn had seen before in the Hall of Animate Retribution, were kept close at hand as their sharp, unrelenting watchdog eyes held constant vigil over the hostages. These were hard men whose profession was to take life. They would not know mercy if she stood right in front of them.

They did not see Jinn in the tent.

And they wouldn't see much of anything for much longer, Jinn thought vindictively.

He lifted his hand and snapped his fingers.

A shroud of white mist arose in the air so quickly the men were still gasping, confused, when the tent was already filled with the blinding vapor. Shrill one-word queries of the hostages came through the air, and the men shouted at them to shut up or they'd die.

Jinn waited no longer before snapping his fingers again.

The growling shouts of the men turned into high-pitched squawks in midsentence.

Even through the obscuring fog, Jinn could see the two men running around scared like a couple of headless chickens—only now they were chickens, with their heads still attached.

Their white feathered wings flapped helplessly as they skittered across the ground with their orange chicken legs, squawking away morosely and incomprehensibly. Jinn grinned in amusement as he watched the show for a few more seconds.

Then he snapped his fingers again, and the plastic bonds holding the scientist hostages prisoner disappeared entirely. Free and unhindered, they began to whisper surreptitiously, not knowing that their guards were in no condition to stop them even if they wanted to.

With another snap Jinn saw to it that the automatic weapons now on the ground turned into licorice and would pose no danger to anyone, not even to a child—well, perhaps in the form of cavities later on.

After making sure the situation was well in hand, Jinn snapped his fingers and vanished before the veiling cloud had a chance to dissipate. As he went, he grinned as he imagined the expressions on their faces when the mist cleared and they were faced with a couple of chickens instead of big men with big guns.

As he made his return to the Hall of Animate Retribution, the mess he'd made with his powers was small in comparison to the true horrors the place presented. Watching calmly as the statues from the niches ran around the chamber hunting down the few remaining mercenaries, Jinn felt oddly not at peace. The curious sensation wouldn't leave him even as he shook his head.

"It's not that easy to shake off your conscience, brother."

Shocked at the familiar feminine voice, Jinn spun around, shaken to the core. She stood amidst all that chaos like a flower in a windy meadow, untouched and unspoiled by the raging elements. Remembering the jasmine scent of her long brown hair on his pillow at dawn as he awoke, and her almond-shaped eyes glimmering mischievously, Jinn was at a loss.

Yes, he'd been aware that it was unlikely he'd be the only genie left in the world. Still, her presence startled him—and the conflicted reaction of pleasure at the sight of a familiar face and the fear of getting whisked away from the two men he'd come to care for frightened him even more.

"Only care for, brother? Surely your heart feels more than that."

"Anayis, it has been a while." Surprised at the calm tone of his voice, Jinn wondered if he had dreamt her.

She smiled playfully, as genies did. As she had always done, so long ago. "I am not a dream, brother."

Jinn grinned. "And you were never my sister, *sister*."

Laughing, she stepped toward Jinn, as naked as the day she had stepped out of the fire. Her slim waist curved above into firm round breasts and below into voluptuous hips, and the bronze hue of her skin was as glowing and youthful as Jinn remembered. He recalled the whispers they had shared in the dark of night, the soft kisses, the exploration of pleasure. So long ago, Jinn thought, and wasn't sure if he felt glum or glad.

"No, I was not, dear brother." Stopping close to him but not close enough to touch, she watched Jinn with fiery eyes—as pandemonium sparked around them. "Why don't you admit what is in your heart... Jinn?"

Frowning at the use of his new name, hearing it clashing against her teeth and lips, was an unpleasant experience for Jinn. "What do you want, Anayis?" There was little point in asking her how she was here, and Jinn knew she would not say. Genies had always been secretive people, even among their own kind.

"I was sent," she replied softly, glancing around at the turmoil but not really seeing it. The golems here were forged in their own fires, and would not attack unless provoked, challenged, or as part of the maze test. "By the Council of Elders." Her late addition was hardly necessary. Jinn had already guessed as much.

"And?" Jinn finally relented to inquire when she withheld her information for a few breaths, too long for comfort or solace. "Why should that concern me? I was ousted by our people. Made a bound genie—"

She scoffed arrogantly, as only genies could. "If you have issues with the decisions of punishment or law, take it up with the Council." Her tone wasn't as harsh as Jinn remembered from the day he'd been sentenced to slavery for the mortal race of men.

"No." Jinn's denial surprised even him. "I have no quarrel with the Council. My punishment was just." Anayis looked up with her brown eyes, curious and more than a little shocked. Clearly she had not expected Jinn's reply, so he added, "Although, in my humble defense, I'd say I have served my time incarcerated. Unless the Council feels I do not deserve my freedom—"

"Is it freedom you seek, brother?" Her smile was wicked again, taunting, just as Jinn recalled. "From what I have observed from my lofty perch you might not mind being bound to these two mortal men with you." For a second Jinn had no answers to offer. "Please, if I am wrong, do correct me."

Admitting the truth was surprisingly easy. "No. You're not wrong." How could he deny it when Pip and Val had given him so much already? And… if the plan forming in the back of his mind succeeded, they would be a part of his life yet again. "He only has one wish left before…." His voice trailed off as he waited for her response, fearing the outcome more than he'd have expected. Before he got to know Pip and Val he might not have minded the Council once again deciding matters against him—but not now. Those two men still needed him—even if only one man lived to be rescued and another needed to be brought safely home for burial.

Anayis smiled softly, empathy flowing from her, and Jinn felt better. "And you wish to know what we, the Council of Elders and the genie populace at large, are going to do about you." Merely nodding, Jinn waited for the female genie to continue. "Nothing. The prince was at fault as much as you were for the… shall we call it an indiscretion? And since the Unveiling…." Momentarily lost in thought, she shrugged and then said, "But, as always, there are rules to adhere to, and believe me, Jinn, they are absolute. They concern your powers."

Jinn swallowed hard—and tried even harder not to show his apprehension. "You and the Council are taking away my powers?"

The teasing chuckle from Anayis was lovelier than he'd remembered, and for a moment all those reasons for having cared for her came flooding back. She shook her head. "Of course not. It would hardly be fair of us to continue punishing you for a transgression so old and unimportant now. No. The rules are as follows: when your wish master has made his last wish, you will be free—unhindered, as the contract clearly states and specifies. When you are free, however, your powers as genie will wane."

Jinn frowned, bewildered. Of all the stories he'd heard about bound genies set free, he had not once heard that their powers had diminished. If anything, they grew stronger. "What do you mean?"

Anayis sighed like the summer breeze, and her eyes were rueful. "The Elders felt the change of the world as the Unveiling approached. They had felt it even before the Age of Enlightenment, when humanity discovered the age of science and reason—though they still have ways to go. Nonetheless, the Elders decreed that no omnipotent powers were allowed anymore for any genies living out among humans. You understand, surely, that because genies are notorious for their rebellious nature against all systems of order, we now must respect this decision. This mandate was, and is, enforced by the gods and their heralds."

That was surprising, Jinn thought. Most gods didn't involve themselves in the day-to-day affairs of mortals, as their attentions lay on the bigger picture. Not that they could, either, as the ban imposed upon them since the dawn of time and space prevented them from direct contact with mortals—even their own devoted worshippers. The temptation to intervene once was bad enough, and after that it would've been like getting an addict to quit an opium habit. "I see."

Anayis grinned mischievously. "Yes, well.... All we genies, bound and not, are held to a higher account now that the world went and changed on us. The Unveiling made sure of that. There's no going back to our former blissful existence where we could wield our powers without fear of divine retribution. Now, it's all mortals this and mortals that." Snorting, she waved her hand about in a telltale gesture of annoyance—and yet sympathy too. "My only consolation is the foreknowledge that, just like all civilizations throughout time, even these pesky little humans will have their day in the sun and then face the music. The omniverse has a habit of striking the proud down a peg or two." At this, she winked at Jinn, who grinned back.

Yes, once upon a time genies had been the most powerful and advanced civilization on Earth. But to all things there was an end, and all that was left of those gilded days of glory were a few embers of scattered genies whose powers waxed and waned with the crests and troughs of mortal men and women who now dominated the world.

This fundamental truth of balance and change might have been a bitter bite to swallow if Jinn had not felt so strongly about two mortals in particular. "So, Anayis, now what?"

At this she laughed, a gust of bubbly sound that warmed Jinn's heart with its familiarity and sincerity. "Oh, Jinn, really. Now you live your own life as *you* wish. I imagine that won't be too difficult for you to have come true, hmm?" Her sisterly scolding was sweet and friendly, and Jinn felt like he'd at long last accepted the reality of his past, come to terms with it, the crimes of passion against his people as he'd willfully and deliberately challenged their leaders. As if she knew what was on his mind, she said, "You do know we could not intercede on your behalf when it came to your punishment, imprisonment, and servitude? The law—"

With a dismissing wave of his hand, Jinn interjected emphatically, "The law was and is just? Yes, I do know that."

His chuckle was met with astonished silence before the beautiful genie said pensively, "Jinn, you've changed. Could it be that your time as a bound genie was good for you?"

Jinn laughed out loud. "I wouldn't go that far, Anayis. However, I… yes, I admit that certain good things have come out of my forcible bondage."

Anayis's brown eyes flashed. "In that case I'm glad and proud that I have not been your jailer but merely your parole officer." To Jinn's obvious confusion, she snickered. "Ah, you are the creation and child of a different era. I just know you will have fun catching up on all things post-Unveiling."

With a wicked wink and a salacious smile, Jinn said, "I'm sure I shall."

"So we come to our second to last bit of business." Anayis's keen eyes observed the continuing bedlam around them. "You are aware that soon all these men will be dead?"

A twinge of pain nudged at the base of Jinn's belly, gnawing on his gut. Despite all that had happened with the mercenaries, Jinn knew turning a blind eye to their inevitable demise in the stone-cold hands of the golems was wrong. He could practically feel the bad karma settling down upon him, and the feeling just made the pinch of guilt that much more obvious, strenuous, and incessant. "Anayis... these men are my enemies. They have already taken the life of one I adore and as a result hurt another I care for. I should want to watch their violent passing into the netherworld. I should relish it."

Anayis's eyes held steadfast, betraying no emotions. "Do you?"

With a deep sigh Jinn had to admit the truth to himself—yet again. "No. They are fools after fool's gold. They are greedy and amoral and cruel. But... death will teach them no lessons. And I do not wish to be responsible for their deaths."

Anayis smiled, content. "Then you know what you need to do to stop their suffering. After all, there has been enough loss." Jinn looked at Anayis. Really looked at her, seeing her as she had been then—and as she was now. There was a new kind of hardness about her, but a sliver of her kind and loving soul came through, like a shard of light piercing the dark. "I have missed you, Jinn. With that in mind I only have one more question to pose: Do you wish to have your name back?"

Jinn's eyes grew wide in sudden shock. No bound genie, even upon release, had been offered their name restored in the annals of genies. The punishment of erasure of the past crimes was set in stone, a permanent fate without reprieve or commutation of sentence. "But... the Council and the law...."

"Times change, Jinn," Anayis said cryptically, apparently unwilling to go into details. "The Council has to accommodate to those adjustments or be rendered obsolete. Your punishment has served its purpose. If you wish it, you can have your name back."

Standing in place, feeling much like a reed bending in the raging wind, almost broken, Jinn stalled for time. For so long he had waited for his freedom and the chance to rebuild his life just as it had been. But now that the opportunity presented itself, Jinn found that he no longer wanted his old life back. All the years of solitude and servitude had taught him that with or without his former name he was still the man who gave the name its meaning.

Pip and Val had given him a name that held a new kind of meaning for him. One he was not ready to dismiss or ignore. Yes, he could go back to the kind of life he'd had, and yes, there would be pleasures. But he wouldn't have Pip and Val then, and—alive or dead—they did still need him.

Him.

Jinn.

Not the man he had been, but the man he was now.

And, unsurprisingly, that was all that really mattered in the end. Yes, Jinn would reinvent himself, and he could do it with the two men who loved him and who he loved back. "Thank you, Anayis, but no thanks. I'm good."

The slightly baffled but more pleased expression Anayis sported was his affirmation. "Even after all these centuries, you still manage to surprise me... Jinn."

After one final tender caress of his cheek, the touch of a friend, lover, and kindred spirit, she was gone.

And Jinn... Jinn was at peace.

With a determined snap of his fingers, he watched quietly, invisible, as the hunting statues stopped, lingered where they stood as they processed their new orders, and then, as silently as the grave, returned to their former niches along the cavern walls.

And the mercenaries, all themselves again after the spells faded, fell on the floor, exhausted and defeated. Jinn snapped his fingers. The expressions of the men went slack, bland, and emotionless. And then the men were gone. The Hall of Animate Retribution might have lived up to its name, but as it stood now it was unnecessary. Balance had been restored, and no more vengeance needed to be exacted upon them.

Mildly, Jinn walked over to the last man still lying on the ground, paralyzed but awake. Yes, but this business still remained unfinished.

TEARY-EYED, his swollen eyes red and heavy-lidded, Val turned to Jinn as he returned, accompanied by a whoosh of air ruffling his hair. But Val didn't really see him. His gaze had turned inward, huddled toward the pain and the sorrow.

Feeling renewed rage encompass him—letting that feeling go would open up the wound that was still too fresh, and the loss would hurt then—Jinn watched the man lying immobile on the ground, only his wide eyes working.

Frowning, Val glanced over his shoulder and found the man lying there, incapacitated. "Who's that?"

"The leader."

Val's reactions were quicker than lightning as he sprung up on his feet and dashed toward the man, growling and yelling like an animal. Jinn stepped forward, got in his way, and grabbed his shoulders. "Váli, no!"

Val struggled to break free. He was really fighting back, tooth and nail. "Let go of me, Jinn! I want to kill him!"

Trying to reason with him, Jinn said, "If he's dead, he won't learn anything."

"I don't care!" Val shouted, and holding him was like attempting to keep a cat in his lap—only this squirming beast was gigantic and furious, out of his mind with grief. "Don't you just want to—"

"Yes, I do, but we're not like him. We're better than him." Jinn let go of the man's shoulders and cupped the sides of his face hard instead, forcing Val to really look at him. Their gazes locked for a breath. "You are better than that, Val. I know you are. You're not like that man. You are a fierce warrior god of the north. Yes, your kind may be a little mischievous and self-absorbed at times"—Val's frowning eyes turned to him in a flash of disbelief and surprise.—"but you are good and honorable guardians because you know it is the responsibility of the strong to protect the weak. And this man is nothing but weak. He deserves not your fury but your pity, for this is all he will ever be. Small and unimportant in the grand scheme of things." Easing his tight hold a smidgen, Jinn smiled softly. "We genies struggle against rules, always have. We hate having to conform to other people's expectations and wishes. We do not want to serve and obey at someone else's leisure."

Val's confused face distorted a bit. "But—"

Jinn's smile was intended as a reassurance, and as Val's furrowed brow smoothed, he felt like he'd accomplished his goal. "You, Val, you and Pip are all I want and need. That you are my wish master is not a cruel and unusual life sentence for me but a privilege I am happy to abide by. Without your kind, Val, the very concepts of honor and dignity and valor would not be the same. You are the most honorable man I know. Pip knows it too, and he wouldn't want you to do this."

Val's handsome face contorted in agony, but the fight in him had gone, and he put up no struggle against Jinn as he pulled him into his embrace. "No... I don't want to be that guy... the one who takes and kills…. But I want to kill him for what he did to us… for what he did to Pip….” All his words came through sobs, slurred and muffled, like those of a child. No amount of experience in life prepared you for the loss of a loved one.

And they didn't have to, either. Jinn leaned back a little to stare Val in the eye with all the love and warmth he'd begun to feel for this man. “Sweetheart, listen to me. You still have wishes left.” His final words came through slow and clear, and he nodded toward Pip lying on the hot ground of the smoke-filled cavern, the roar of flames all around them.

Val's eyes followed Jinn's gaze down, and then shot back up, wide with shock—and hope. “Y-you can really do that…?”

Jinn smiled in relief and let out a near-sobbing breath of his own. “I can do anything you wish, sweetheart. *Anything*.” The pointed look he gave could not have been misconstrued, and luckily Val seemed to understand.

Breathing so fast he was almost out of breath and probably seeing spots in his dizzying field of vision, Val mumbled, “Revive Pip. No! I wish he had not been shot at all.”

“As you wish.”

As freely as genies could interpret wishes and their execution, in this instance Jinn had no doubts about how to proceed. Snapping his fingers, he gently pressed his palm over Val's chest where his heart beat so fast it felt like it might tear out of him. Pushing the former god back for his own good and safety, Jinn watched as Pip's body shook.

It was as though reality was something tangible that condensed and ground to a complete halt around them, as though the cavern's walls drew closer to them, as though all of space-time existed in between heartbeats. The fires stopped roaring, the smoke hung heavy and motionless in the air, and all sounds were suppressed as time stood still. The only people in the world were Jinn and Val and Pip in this instant when time itself blinked.

Gasping, Val too watched as Pip's body moved up from the ground. Only he didn't do it on his own. As though the snap of Jinn's fingers had found the remote control for time and hit rewind, Pip got up in exactly the reverse of falling down.

And then the bullet came out the same way it had gone in.

The red smudge on Pip's shirt disappeared as the deadly bullet hovered in midair right in front of him. The faint echo of the gunshot reflected around the cavern walls, ringing in Jinn's ears as it had before, only backward. Air rippled around the frozen high-velocity projectile, like an arrow piercing water, moving in infinitesimal increments away from Pip—who was suddenly blinking fiercely, alive and well, death leaving him in the form of an actual bullet.

"What...?" Pip's voice was baffled but so alive.

Val's eyes hung on the bullet cutting through the air, stilled in motion against all the laws of physics. Without a word, Val plucked the bullet from midair, holding it in his shaky fingers as if that one piece of metal was his worst enemy.

A whoosh of thick, smoke-filled air rushed at them as the flames around the chamber began to light up again. Time resumed its regularly scheduled flow in the blink of an eye.

And there was Pip, alive and confused. "What on earth...? I thought.... Wasn't I—"

His intended queries were cut short when Val hurriedly crossed the gap between them and hugged the young man within an inch of his life. Pip oomphed but embraced Val in return, resting his cheek against the man's chest with a contented sigh. "Oh, love, I thought I lost you," Val whispered, his voice shaky.

"What?" Frozen in his bewilderment, Pip asked the question, but his voice was muffled by Val's body surrounding him until he relaxed again and let himself be held.

Silently sobbing, Val turned his teary gaze to Jinn, who couldn't keep the cracking smile off his lips or prevent his vision blurring with the swelling of tears. "Thank you, Jinn. By all the gods in the known omniverse, thank you." He straightened his arm in a needy, inviting gesture. Jinn took his hand, and Val yanked him into a three-way bear hug, nearly crushing all of them together in his furiously feverish, desperate embrace. Whispering, *"Thank you,"* over and again against Jinn's neck, Val was overcome with emotion, and Jinn comforted him by encircling the two men with his own big arms. Val's fears had been Jinn's fears, as palpable and concrete as any he'd ever felt, and the idea of never seeing Pip's hazel eyes sparkle again, of never seeing that heart-warming blush again, of never feeling the love Pip had to offer—it was all too much to contemplate any further.

"Who's that?" Pip's words came out muted and distorted due to having his mouth full of clothing and muscle, sounding more like *whoof aff.*

Both Jinn and Val broke the group hug, looking back where the man was still lying on the ground, flanked by clouds of smutty smoke and the heat of fires, his skin dirty and sweaty. The tiny round glasses perched on his nose were crooked, and his expression was blank, but his eyes showed his fear—and his greed, as he couldn't take his eyes off the jinn, who felt no more hate for this man now that Pip was back, alive and safe with them. This small, pathetic man, engulfed in his vices, was not worth wasting any more of Jinn's precious time.

"I heard all the other men, the mercenaries, speak or cry out as they met their fate, except this man. And the way they tried to defend him suggests he's the man holding the purse strings—and the one who spoke to you, Pip, through the intercom. One of the mercenaries confirmed this. Mr. Smith, I believe. The leader." Jinn kept his tone matter-of-fact to prevent any heated emotional reactions.

But Pip was still confused, and Val had gotten hold of his rage by now. "What's that gooey gunk all over him?" Val asked, pointing at the man's wet face and upper body.

Jinn grinned devilishly. "Saliva and venom." Both Val and Pip shot their gazes at him, and he smiled calmly. "He was in the Lair of the Giant Serpent when I whisked him away to the Hall of Animate Retribution. Wrong place to be if you don't want to get eaten. The venom acts as a paralytic while the Giant Serpent devours you—or, in this case, him. Unintentionally, I saved his life. Yet I doubt when that potent substance wears off he'll be in a rush to thank me for it." Jinn crossed his arms over his chest, knowing very well how powerful that stance made him look at his colossal size—even if he was wearing nothing but jeans. And sure enough, the shadow of terror glimpsed on his face was a telltale sign of Jinn's effect on lesser men.

"I know him."

That sudden statement caught both Val and Jinn off guard as Pip's small but composed voice spoke. "How?" Val was quick to demand an answer and an explanation.

Pip's pouting lips accompanied the shake of his head and the reproachful glare he shot in Val's direction. "Oh, Val, you really can be so blind sometimes. We've both met him. He was at the foundation's annual conference in London last year. In fact, I think he's been to all of them. He's a benefactor."

Val's blue eyes flashed in anger. "That's not the word I'd choose," he grumbled.

"Who is he?" Jinn interjected with his soothing tranquility.

"Oh, what was his name…?" Pip's brow furrowed, and he bit his lip in deep concentration, working through his memory. "He funds the foundation to an extent. If I remember correctly, he's a collector of antiquities. Oh, oh, now I remember! Winston Watson!"

"Seriously?" Val asked, incredulous, a disgusted look on his face. Jinn suppressed a chuckle, acknowledging the former Viking god's taste for esthetics. But then Val's expression changed as recollection dawned on him and his eyes went wide. "Yes, I *do* remember him too. Watson. He came to my lecture on the Babylonian goddess Ishtar."

"Great lecture," Pip whispered to Jinn from his side, staring at Val dreamily. Jinn doubted he'd intended for Val to hear him, but in the hollow space of the large cavern his hushed voice carried. Val smiled smugly and winked, and Pip blushed all over, biting his lower lip in dazed adoration.

"Collector of antiquities, eh?" Jinn looked down at the man, who had not moved from his spot and who hadn't made even the tiniest noise. "I'm going to tell you a story, little man, so listen carefully." Hunkering down, he inspected the helpless, evil man from head to toe. "I'm afraid your timing could not have been more unfortunate. For you see, Mr. Watson, as the Unveiling, as you call it, has at long last truly come to pass, what was formerly unseen is now visible. No longer must the jinn remain hidden from either world." Now Jinn smiled. "As a lamp genie, I was bound by ancient law to grant Pip, my lovely liberator and delectable wish master, three glorious, once-in-a-lifetime wishes. However… upon completion of set tasks and my contractual duties, I have now been set free, bound by that accursed lamp—or wishes of mortals—no more."

Pip's eyebrows shot up in surprised shock. "Really?"

"Indeed, dear boy." Jinn turned calmly to the man lying impotent and vulnerable on the ground. "So you see, little human, you're out of luck—and out of genies." Yes, he'd left out the part that Pip had not had the chance to make all his wishes and that Jinn had a new wish master now. For all he knew Watson had already figured all that out since he'd seen Val make the wish to bring Pip back to life. But it did not matter. "And now, Mr. Watson, in order to protect my charges, and anyone else, from your infinite greed, I have been granted the right to ensure you do not pose a further problem. I do hope you got a good look at the genies here, because you will not remember them for much longer."

After tapping Watson's forehead, Jinn snapped his fingers. Behind his spectacles, the man's eyes glazed over, and a peaceful, relaxed expression forced out the greedy malice. As his memory of all things genie evaporated from his mind as though they had never been there at all, Jinn snapped his fingers one last time.

And what remained of the collector/evil mastermind about to have a change of lifestyle vanished without a sound. Like his private army suffering from acute amnesia, he too would wake up unharmed in his own bed far away, with no memory of genies and magical oil lamps, of mercenaries and murders—and he'd have this uncontrollable urge to donate most of his vast fortune to charity. Jinn smiled. Yes, that seemed fitting. He knew he was taking liberties with his license to use his powers to protect himself and his wish masters, but as far as he was concerned, this fell into the category of necessities for survival.

"Where is he? What'd you do to him?" Val's voice was cold and stark, and Jinn knew he didn't care if the man was dead or alive. But he sought assurances that Watson would not trouble them again.

"I sent him home—without his memory of recent events and with an unimpeachable sudden need to donate his fortune to the less fortunate."

For a moment there was a stunned silence.

Then…. "Oh, Jinn. That was positively brilliant." Pip's sweet voice held all the warmth and reassurance Jinn needed to know he'd done the right thing by not killing the man outright. Yes, he could have, but, just like he'd told Val, Jinn was not like that. In admiration and adoration, Pip launched himself at Jinn, hugging him to bits.

Resting his chin on Pip's sandy hair, Jinn felt contented and connected, and he embraced the smaller man with all his might, nearly crushing him in the process. He feared to let go as he worried something bad would happen, and not even the happy humming coming from Pip completely alleviated those anxieties.

"He's right, Jinn. I don't think I could've been so generous and forgiving. It was the right thing to do. To let him live. Him and his men."

Val smiled at him softly, and Jinn knew Val shared all his fears of losing someone he loved. Someone like Pip. Val came to him then, that sexy, charming smile on those picture-perfect lips, and joined the embrace, allowing himself to be pulled tight and close. Wrapping his arms around both men, Jinn finally felt like it was all going to be all right. As long as they were together, no force in the omniverse could tear them apart.

Then Pip's small voice came from below his chin. "Does anyone know where the elevator back to the surface is, or should we just make ourselves comfortable here?"

And at that, both Jinn and Val roared into laughter, not even needing to see Pip blush.

Chapter Ten

HIS feet tired and worn out even through the strong soles of his shoes, Val managed to take the last few remaining steps toward the deluxe suite at the Westbury, the five-star luxury hotel in Mayfair London, where he was staying with Pip and Jinn for three nights following their long trip from Oman the day before. The foundation had been kind enough to fund their brief stay there. Last night they'd all been too tired to do anything more than crash on the bed and sleep.

Not bothering to silence the weary sigh or the yawn that followed, Val closed the door behind him, dropped his laptop bag and other assorted bags on the floor, and made his way to the luxurious bedroom with its king-size bed he couldn't wait to fall on.

What he found instead was a happy, bouncy Pip hopping on their bed, which remarkably didn't give out even the mildest squeak. He was wearing nothing but his natural white boxers and a tight white T-shirt. And damn if he didn't look delicious, all giddy and giggling.

"What are you doing?" he asked, amused, stopping at the foot of the bed.

Pip grinned wickedly. "Being a brat."

"Oh, yeah? Well... knock it off."

"Make me!" Pip laughed, and Val really loved seeing the young man of his dreams so very full of life. Val had seen him in the opposite of this current elation, and he would've done anything to make sure it never happened again. "Besides... what did you expect me to do with you leaving me here all by my lonesome to entertain myself?" To emphasize his point, Pip grabbed his prick through his boxers, and a flash of heat shot down Val's spine and pooled in the pit of his belly and in his boiling groin. His cock grew erect so fast it almost hurt.

Val smiled. "If you'll give me a sec to take a shower and wash up, I'll make sure you don't have to play with just yourself anymore. How does that sound?" Pip's gleeful shout was answer enough, and Val began to unbutton the sapphire-blue formal dress shirt he'd worn for the meeting at Oxford.

"How'd the meeting go?" Pip asked, refusing to come down from his hopping heights despite the seriousness of the topic.

Val shrugged calmly and went to work on his belt buckle and zipper. "Boring. Long. Heated—as in poor air-conditioning." Shucking the shirt and the belt away, Val continued quietly, frowning. "They accepted our version of events without contestation. Not that there's anyone around to contradict us, since Jinn did his thing. Worrying about what was hidden underneath the city, the foundation's closing the site down for at least six months to assess the level of threat to future expeditions, or so they put it, anyway. But considering we've been down there and seen the dangers for ourselves, they're expecting full accounts and official statements from us, anything that can help them with their security assessment of the location and establishing surveillance parameters. Their words. So we're going to be pretty busy from now on. But... I was, however, able to get us accepted on the roster of the next expedition to the site, so we'll be running things there, or at least be the leading experts there—"

"All of us?" Pip interjected, his hazel eyes burning and sharp with the query.

Val smiled and nodded. Glad that they had their genie to accompany them, he recalled the snap of Jinn's fingers when he'd come up with a fake passport and ID for his new official self. *Jinn Jones.* That had to be the most ridiculous false identity in the history of faux personalities. Val had thought he'd spit out his tea or choke as he listened to Jinn enthusiastically explaining his new identity to an equally amused Pip, coming to the conclusion that falsified documents were such a vital requirement that they necessitated using his powers, for continued survival, as Jinn called it. "Oh, please," Val had muttered to himself, and Jinn's wicked wink had been affirmation enough. "Yes, love. All *three* of us." After the confirmation, Val looked around, curious. "Where is Jinn?"

"He's taking a bath. In the Jacuzzi."

Val sighed. "Again?"

Pip shrugged but smiled salaciously. "The guy really loves his Jacuzzi. And he said he still had sand everywhere—but I'm beginning to think that's just an excuse." He winked at Val, who chuckled in response. Yes, after all those baths, Jinn had to be cleanest genie in the world. Although he was the *only* genie they knew of so....

By then Val had removed most articles of clothing, but to his own nose he smelled too ripe to play with Pip yet. "The shower's free, though, right?" A shower stall with ample room was adjacent to the whirlpool bathtub currently occupied by the colossal genie.

"Yep. Want some company?" Pip waggled his eyebrows, his pink tongue peeking out between his teeth as he grinned. "Want me to wash your back?"

Wearing only his dark-blue boxer briefs, Val chuckled and got up on the bed in front of the bouncing boy. "Somehow I doubt that'd be the end of it, don't you agree?" Pip stopped bouncing and snaked his arms around Val's neck, rising up on his toes to kiss Val, whose blood began to roar in his veins. His heart thudded almost out of his chest, and his cock stood up in salute, painfully hot and hard as he wrapped his arms around Pip's waist and yanked him close. They kissed heatedly, hungrily, and Val had a hard time holding onto his self-control. He wanted inside Pip now, not ten minutes from now.

"Hey, you two. Starting without me?" Jinn's amused voice came from the bathroom doorway, and both Val and Pip turned to watch the gigantic naked man lean against the doorframe, his muscles quivering beneath the sun-kissed skin. Well, he wasn't entirely naked, as he had a towel wrapped around his waist, riding low on both his hips and his knees. Still, the tented towel was proof positive of his state of arousal.

"Fuck…," Val mumbled, knowing he'd miss out on too much if he took that two minutes' worth of a damn shower.

Jinn apparently read his growling wrong, because his smile faltered, and the bulge on his groin began to go down. "Or perhaps you two would like to be left alone?" He began to turn around to step back into the bathroom, and Val felt his blood run cold with sudden fear.

Pip cured him of that in a heartbeat, beating Val to it. "Jinn, listen to me." Pip flumped down on the bedspread, his serious gaze aimed at Jinn, who turned around to hear what he had to say. Val saw a grain of fear there, deep within those electric-blue eyes he'd come to adore as much as Pip's hazel eyes, and he wanted that uncertainty to go away for good. "Right from the start you've been like a rock to us, strong and steadfast. I knew I could trust you from the get-go because you are pure of heart. Time and again you've shown us your true character—brave, intelligent, and unyielding. You saved my life, revived me when I was gone. You saved Val's life—and his honor when he was about to do something horrific. We don't want you to stay—" Val gasped and felt like he'd entered the *Twilight Zone* just before Pip finished his sentence. "—just out of gratitude. I love you, Jinn." Val swallowed, blinking away tears, and saw Jinn's massive body quiver too. "I know I don't have any more wishes left because I, you know, died and all, but from the bottom of my heart I wish you would stay, Jinn. That you'd *want* to stay with us as much as we want you to stay. Right, Val?"

His throat inaccessible due to the emotional lump there, Val merely nodded. Hurriedly, he scrambled off the bed toward the bathroom door, pulled Jinn into his arms, and hugged the breath out of him. Not an easy feat considering Jinn was about four inches taller than Val, but he managed.

"I love you too, Jinn," he murmured against the genie's neck, kissing the tanned skin there, smooth and soft, yet underneath lay hidden less-than-surprising strength. Moving back when he felt Jinn's muscular arms wind around his waist, Val smiled tenderly—and then mischievously, causing Jinn's eyes to flash with suspicion. "Pip may not have any more wishes left—but I do. One. Last. Wish. I wish you were naked, Jinn. Not all the time, mind you. But for now, right at this moment, here with us. I wish you were naked."

"Oh, Val, that's a superb wish...," Pip sighed from the bed, and Val glanced back over his shoulder at him, finding Pip sitting on the edge of the bed, his gaze glued on the two of them—and his hand in his boxers, stroking his dick. Val heard himself make a strange choked sound, like a cough or, dare he say it, a gurgle.

Jinn smiled, and the look of him was smooth and easy and beautiful again. "As you wish, master." And without warning he dropped his towel from around his waist to the floor. He didn't even need to snap his fingers, Val noted amusedly, but then he saw the picture-perfect masculine specimen before him and could no longer form a coherent thought.

The great thing about the situation was that he didn't need to take even a step forward to reach Jinn. With his palms, Val explored the vast and firm expanses of Jinn's chest, the silky smooth skin without imperfections of any kind, feeling the genie's heartbeat accelerating as his palms shifted and moved all over, tracing curves of muscles and lines of skin. "Wasn't that cheating a bit? You didn't have to use your powers to grant my wish."

"You're right, master," Jinn purred, although because he was such a big beefy man the sound reverberated more like a growl, but either way, to Val it was a sensuous, exciting sound akin to the sweet angelic voice of his beloved Pip. Their unique voices began to blend together into a symphony of love until he couldn't say where his excitement, want, and love for Pip ended and the same for Jinn began. "Make your wish, then."

While pinching Jinn's perfect brown nipples into hard nubs sticking out wantonly, Val didn't hesitate. "I wish to give my last wish to Pip." The last few words came out muffled as he moved suddenly to sucking Jinn's right nipple into his mouth, tonguing all around, and applying just a graze from his teeth. Jinn shuddered, and Val gloated a little with pride at his sexy accomplishment.

Suddenly Pip was there at his side, whispering naughty things in his ear. "Do it, Val. Mark him for the both of us."

Val was happy to oblige, encircling Jinn's nipple with his mouth and latching on until he'd suckled so hard he knew there'd be a bruise there the next day. Jinn shivered, and his powerful arms surrounded Val. The beating of his heart sped up through his feverish skin. Val lavished more of his undivided attention on Jinn as he slid his mouth over to the left nipple, and suddenly he felt Pip at his side, his cheek close to his so that the hairs on the back of his neck stood up with the electricity of the sensuous intimacy. He heard more than saw the wet suckling Pip inflicted on Jinn's right nipple, and set to work raising Jinn's left tight little nub of flesh to a hardened state. Jinn groaned, and Val smiled against his chest, Jinn's arms tightening around him. *Touchdown.*

But all of a sudden Pip pushed those forceful arms away and laughed playfully. "Na-ah. Not yet, big guy. Val has to take a shower first."

Val wasn't quite sure if he was angry over the interruption of his happy meal or grateful, since he did feel dirty—and not in the good way—next to these two clean, sweet-scented guys. Lifting his head from Jinn's chest and licking his lips, he nodded. "Right." Reluctantly, Val let go of the genie, whose electric-blue eyes shone darker now, filling Val with hitherto unknown depths of hunger. "Don't start anything too hot without me," he managed to mutter huskily before dashing past Jinn to the bathroom and closing the door.

In the privacy of the steamy hot room with white marble everywhere, Val admitted to himself how much he wanted this. Not just the sex with his forever beloved Pip and newly discovered beloved Jinn, but to build the foundation of a relationship with them. Something that could last beyond the passion and the need and extend outside the sheets of the bed and the walls of the bedroom. Val wanted their love as much as he longed to give his to them. And recalling the loving feeling of warmth, closeness, and intimacy he'd shared with Pip and Jinn over the past few days, Val knew he was on his way to getting there.

WHILE watching Val retreat into the soothing ambience of the bathroom, Pip thought about how they'd gotten here. After the underground city incident, as he liked to call it, there'd been briefings with the foundation via webcams as well as light interrogations by the local law enforcement—though for Pip they had seemed too hard to call lightweight. There'd been far too many conversations and interviews, debates and inquiries to make him relax. He'd spouted out the story so many times by now that he knew the proper wordings in his sleep. Getting all the scientists as well as the site workers to safety had been their secondary concern, as the primary was securing the safety of the genie.

My genie. Jinn.

Back sitting on the edge of the bed, Pip turned his face to watch Jinn combing his long black hair, standing there as exposed as Val had wished him to be. Broad shoulders, strong back, lean waist, round buttocks, powerful thighs, long legs…. Struggling to keep still, Pip was losing his mind. Yes, it would be inappropriate for him to start the proceedings with Jinn without Val there, but every second he spent admiring the gigantic, muscular form of Jinn, displayed before him like a bronze statue of a god, he was one heartbeat closer to succumbing to his urges.

With his back to Pip, Jinn chuckled. "Maybe you ought to join Val in a cold shower, Pip, if you lack—"

"I'm fine… meanie," Pip replied, huffing in less-than-righteous indignation, because he wasn't fine by any standards.

Throwing his wild mane about, more for effect than drying, and laughing out loud, Jinn turned, winked at Pip shamelessly, and leisurely walked over to him. All Pip could see was the huge cock bopping before him, dark brown all over, jutting out from a nest of black pubes, and the scent of male musk and sandalwood grew stronger in Pip's nose as he closed his eyes and inhaled.

It wasn't until his cheek nudged the wet tip of said cock that Pip realized he'd leaned over. Startled, he jumped back, his face reheating to the point he felt like he might burn up. "I…. You…. Didn't mean to…."

"Oh, go on, Pip. Give it a lick. You and I both know you want to."

Pip nearly broke his neck craning it around Jinn's body to see Val walking up to them from the bathroom amidst a cloud of steam. Only wearing a white towel around his hips, while drying his golden-brown hair on another towel, Val looked delicious to Pip, his chest strewn with flaxen blond hair, and a similar hued trail sprinkled down from his belly button toward the rim of the towel. Val sauntered closer with a wicked grin on his luscious lips.

"I hate you…," Pip said, pouting and frowning, wrinkling his pretty little nose in disapproval of being the object of continuous taunting by these two drop-dead gorgeous men.

"No, you don't." Val chuckled, leaning down to kiss him, and Pip was ready to come right then and there. "You love me."

Val glanced at Jinn, and the two of them exchanged a look that had Pip near climbing the walls with curiosity, like sitting on an anthill. Jinn looked down at Pip, who quivered under the heated stare. "Get in the middle of the bed."

There wasn't a chance in the world Pip was going to protest the order, so he scurried off to the bed, landing against the softly padded emerald-green headboard with a thud as his back made contact. He had to bite his lip to prevent crying out at the sheer pleasure of watching two gorgeous men who loved and wanted him climbing after him onto the bed like two predators, occupying both sides of him with perfectly toned bodies radiating heat and emanating lust in waves.

"What shall we do with our little Pip first?" Jinn teased.

When Val devilishly grinned back at the genie, Pip felt like he was coming undone in his arousal, and his pink prick, that lay heavily on his belly, twitched at the numerous possibilities of what three men could do together running through his feverish mind. "I think our tasty little morsel should be savored, don't you?" Val said.

Jinn grinned back almost perversely. "Mmm, I like the way you think, dear boy." The fact that he spoke with a perfect high-class English accent only made him sound lewder.

Whatever protests might have entered Pip's imagination evaporated when these two beautiful and strong men lowered themselves at his sides, pulling him further down on the bed, their fingers and palms caressing and stroking on the way down, and their lips and tongues acquainting themselves with the salty and musky natural flavor of Pip's skin. Caught in a daze, Pip whimpered when two hands belonging to two different men fisted his cock and two sets of lips devoted themselves to his pleasure.

Pip had to close his eyes because his brain couldn't handle both the image of two hot naked guys working him and the sensation, so wholly alien to him he practically sobbed with the flush of emotions. "Oh... my... God...."

Val chuckled against Pip's prick, and the hot breath and the vibrations made Pip moan loudly. "I do believe our lovely little boy likes this."

Jinn lifted his head too and laughed, saying in his smooth, sultry tone, "Do you, Pip? Do you like our ministrations? You want more?"

"Oh, please, *yes*," Pip whispered, his hips bucking up to reach for any sort of contact, or friction, or touch.

"As you wish." Jinn chuckled and lowered his head to suckle on the pretty pink crown of Pip's prick, fastening his lips just around the ridge and devouring the head with fierce suction, sweet licks, and soft, insistent pressure against the slit. Pip could not see any of this, but he felt it all, and whatever was left of his rational mind vacated the building.

"Yes, as you wish, love," Val echoed, and he ran the flat of his tongue up from the base of the cock until his tongue touched Jinn's lips, but then his mouth glided back down, giving wet yet intense openmouthed kisses all along the length of the shaft. Pip felt the hot breath of Val's mouth fanning over his dick, now wet with saliva and precome, and the throbbing within increased tenfold. Without a shred of doubt, he knew he'd never felt so much pleasure in his whole life, had never felt so loved, adored, and desired as he did now, and was well aware that without these two men his life would be empty and hollow and all he would have to fill his lonely nights would be memories of this.

"Please…," he murmured, feeling the need course through his veins like liquid fire, thumping to the drumming beat of his heart.

"You need to come, love?" Val's breathy whisper was hoarse, and when Pip glanced down at him, he saw that two blue eyes that usually were the color of bright summer skies had now darkened to stormy dark-blue clouds that threatened to ravage the land beneath. And Pip was most certainly underneath the man, and in his present condition, he could only nod weakly. "Shall we give our sweet lover a reprieve?" Val asked Jinn, who lifted his head from Pip's cock, and his full, luscious lips were bright red and swollen like ripe apples, gaining even more moisture as his tongue swiped across them.

Jinn grinned, his breath heavy too. "I think we shall. Come on, then, Váli. Let's suck our little Pip dry."

"Little…?" Pip mumbled, wanting to sound hurt, but when two mouths returned to take his cock, he no longer cared what particular term of endearment they chose to describe him by. Now there were two darted tongues sampling and snatching his precome, licking around the head while swiping touches of each other as well. Pip closed his eyes in sensory rapture.

Then someone moved further down on his cock, past the base to nuzzle, lick, and suck on his testicles, lapping them and suckling on them, and Pip was certain his head would come clean off. It felt as if there were a thousand fingers, a hundred hands, and a dozen mouths devoted solely to his pleasure, all over him, taking him beyond all that he knew into uncharted and unexplored territory. The suction on his cock and on his balls tightened, and he wiggled, moaning, unable to keep still. Then the two mouths switched places, and Pip didn't care who did what as long as it went on forever. Licks on his perineum and bites on his inner thighs just confirmed his belief this was a pure, unadulterated paradise of pleasure.

But when the wet slurping sound turned to wet smacks and hungry groaning, and his cock cooled, neglected, Pip rose up on his elbows to watch the scene play out. Pip wished secretly he had a camera to capture this rare moment in time and space when he saw the two men he cared about most in the world succumb to a starving kiss.

It was too hot for words. There wasn't even a trace of jealousy, annoyance, or frustration in Pip's heart and body as he silently observed every nibble of lip with teeth, every lick of tongues, every gasp devoured. His own appetite grew to immeasurable heights, and he knew he could've watched Val and Jinn kissing all night long. With a barely audible contented sigh, he surrounded his saliva-and-precome-dripping cock with his hand and began to pump.

Typically he had to close his eyes and dream of Val or another man to get off, as his own eyes and hand just felt inadequate without the imaginary component. But now he had two live, very real, and extremely sexy guys kissing—really kissing—in front of him, hovering above his hot cock, and he needed nothing more. The sight of them together, the still lingering feel of two hands and tongues on his most sensitive organ, and the emotional bond he had with Val and Jinn were all he wanted and needed.

"Hey, we were there first."

Val's hand landed over Pip's hand on his cock and vehemently squeezed to stop him. Pip shuddered and gasped at the sudden strength of it. And the man had, for all intents and purposes, growled his words out.

Jinn's huge palm joined Val's, and he too made a fierce grumbling sound as he spoke. "No playing with yourself without us, remember?"

Pip blushed all over when Val and Jinn looked straight at him, scolding him with their fiery eyes. Then both men pushed up, as if on silent, unanimous cue, and covered his flanks with their writhing bodies, so smoldering hot and shaky that Pip's cock jumped under the two palms surrounding him.

Then Val kissed him, hotly and hungrily, demanding entry with a fervent push of his tongue, and Pip complied eagerly, opening up and letting himself be swallowed up. Before he could fully process the sensation of kissing and being kissed by Val, his dream man, Pip felt a nudge at his jaw when Jinn's strong fingers guided him away from the kiss—and into a new kiss with Jinn.

And it was perfect. Pip sighed into the kiss as his hand began to rise up. He'd wanted to do it for so long that he could no longer deny himself. Pip threaded his fingers through the thick, long mane of Jinn's silky black hair that tickled his skin, and wrapped the long strands around his fingers, tugging. The sweet scent of jasmine blossoms exuding from Jinn's hair disarmed all his defenses, and he let go with a strangled moan.

Suddenly Pip felt a lick on the side of his mouth, testing how tight the latching of two pairs of lips were. Jinn moved back just a hairbreadth, and then Val's tongue was right there to replace Jinn's. And then there were two tongues dueling and dancing together to breach Pip's lips and move in, and he let them, surrendering to the multitude of sensations born out of the threefold kiss.

In so many ways this was a day of revelations for him. New experiences were created by the company of Val and Jinn left and right, and Pip had no knowledge beyond that he wanted all of this to continue into infinity.

The differences in kissing styles were curious but not overwhelming as the two men tended to complement each other as if born to the practice. Where Val was ardent and demanding in his hunger, like a wild beast, Jinn was sensuously slower, more deliberate and controlled, taking his time to explore and savor all that Pip had to offer. Pip could understand why that was as Val was finally united with his destined love, needing the connection more than air itself, while Jinn had already in life succumbed to his desires and lived his life wantonly but had learned his lesson in temperance and patience, progressing at a prolonged pace more suited for him now. And Pip in the middle stood, or lay, as the nexus between the two gorgeous lovers, connecting all of them into a love triangle of equals in perfect harmony.

We belong together. Pip sighed happily into the kiss.

Both Val and Jinn drew back, breaking the intense kiss, causing shivers down Pip's spine and frustration at his unfulfilled need. Both men chuckled low, exchanging another knowledgeable glance as though they had been partners in crime for ages instead of only a few days.

"Yes, love, we sure do," Val remarked with a soft smile tugging his lips.

"Oh, we so absolutely do," Jinn confirmed on Pip's other side, a grin on his curvaceous lips.

Only then did Pip realize he'd said that out loud, breathed it into the kiss, sharing his innermost thoughts and emotions in one sentence he'd exhaled without being consciously aware of it. Yet he knew it was true—and apparently Jinn and Val felt the same. It had become crystal clear to him a while back that there was no escaping how he felt about Val and Jinn, as they encompassed the most minute details of his life. His thoughts wandered over to Jinn's grin when he was taking a shower or to Val's blue eyes when he lay half-awake in his bed at night. The scent of their skin in his nostrils, the feel of their hands around him, their voices whispering to him at all hours of the day. Pip was, for all intents and purposes, theirs.

He had to bite his lower lip to keep it from trembling and blink severely to hold back the tide of tears threatening to break through. "I love you." Yes, his soft voice did crack at the frantic swelling of emotions within him, but Pip knew it didn't matter. His heart was safe with Val and Jinn.

Jinn leaned down again, slanting his mouth and covering Pip's lips with his own. Soon Val's lips joined in, and once more three mouths sought each other heatedly, three tongues entwining and entangling as one, their hot breaths mingling. It was by far the most sensual and sexual experience Pip had ever known, and the impending dawn became just a dream. For tonight was theirs, and theirs alone.

AGAIN Jinn broke the kiss first.

He wanted more from both Pip and Val, and the kissing had done nothing to soothe the aching need within him. In fact, it had merely ignited his slow kindling flame of arousal into a roaring wildfire of sexual need.

"No."

Jinn's eyes widened at the raspy command Pip uttered, and he felt a similar reaction from Val at his side. But he knew where the plea came from. The deep-rooted desire that knew no boundaries and respected no restraints. "Soon, honey." He turned to Val. "Pip's your true love, and has been since time immemorial. You should be the first to love him."

Val nodded, but quickly his hand landed on Jinn's arm, even as Jinn attempted to withdraw further back to let the two enjoy their first time together. But Val's hold was adamant. "Yes, but... I want you to be inside of me while I fuck Pip. Will you?" For the second time in mere moments, Jinn felt flabbergasted. "That way we will all three of us be connected to each other, and you and I will both love Pip."

Underneath them Pip gasped, and Jinn didn't need to look at him to know he was both aroused and blushing all over. A small whimper of desperation aired out of him right after, and Val grinned, but his gaze too was directed elsewhere—at Jinn.

And then Jinn knew exactly how their sexy liaison would play out from here on. "Yes."

Without waiting for Val to take the lead, Jinn jumped up on his feet, grabbed Val by his hips, lifted him up, and placed him gently down on top of Pip, in between Pip's splayed legs, which trembled faster than his heaving chest. Watching the two men ease into each other, finding the right fit and aligning their respective body parts, was a powerful aphrodisiac to Jinn, who palmed his own cock and stroked softly. It wasn't time yet to come.

Looking past Val's shoulder at Pip, Jinn smiled seductively. "You know, Pip, you still have one more wish. The one Val granted you."

Leaning on his elbow, Val shifted on top of Pip to place his upper torso out of the way so he could watch both Pip and Jinn. "That's right, love. So, what are you going to wish for? You'll have a hard time topping my wish to get Jinn all naked and comfy and cozy." Val's bright, insinuating smile caused Pip's eyes to flutter, and his pale chest took on a pinkish hue.

Jinn dropped down on his knees, Pip's right leg caught between his massive tree-trunk-like thighs, and rubbed his huge balls against the soft, hairless skin of Pip's thigh. Pip panted, and his hazel eyes grew wide, and then darkened to brown caramel as his pupils dilated. Jinn loved the look of him like this, so amorous, desirous, and wanton, and he couldn't wait to find out what this young mortal had in mind for his final wish.

But as his recent experiences after having been called from the oil lamp had proven, Jinn was in for yet another surprise.

"That necklace...." Pip pointed at the black leather strap that surrounded Jinn's neck skintight, a gruesome memory of his incarceration and of his many indiscretions. "It's a sign of your forced servitude and ownership by a mortal, isn't it?"

Jinn's eyes narrowed, and despite his conscious thoughts running around like electrical currents, his erection began to wilt as a result of the serious conversational topic, but then it suddenly jumped as Pip's genius excited him. "Yes, you're right—as usual. You're a clever man, Pip. I'm impressed." And he was too. There was a lot about Pip that had Jinn all hot and bothered—his intelligence, observational skills, and natural curiosity being at the forefront. Not excluding his physical beauty, his slim stem of a pale body glowing like a precious pearl or a silvery gem in the form of a young human male.

Pip's eyes flashed, and he blinked away the tears there. He drew his lips into a thin white line and lifted his chin a little, indicating his determination. "I wish you to destroy it, to be free of wish masters. Right now."

Unable to contain the surge of love and admiration from within his soul toward Pip, Jinn smiled, pouring every fragile and overwhelming emotion in his heart into that earnest gesture. "As you wish... my love."

And Jinn snapped his fingers one last time for a wish master.

The black leather collar, the mark of an indentured genie, vanished into thin air.

For a fleeting moment, Jinn felt like he was naked. Not physically nude, but emotionally exposed, and it was all because the constricting piece of wish master/genie bondage had been removed from him. A weight had been lifted from his shoulders, a weight the size of the world. Brushing his fingers over his neck and throat, free of all signs of eternal contractual obligations, he couldn't wrap his brain around the reality of it choking his throat with a lump and causing his lungs to burn with the intensity of it.

Breathing heavily to catch his lost breath, Jinn finally focused his gaze from inward introspection to outward sensations—and Pip. "How... how did you know what my collar meant?"

Pip's sympathetic eyes glistened with a coat of fresh tears, and he smiled softly. "It was the only thing you wore when you appeared before me in your birthday suit." Jinn loved Pip's kind voice emanating from his empathetic, loving soul, and knew he adored him more than anyone ever in his life—mortal and immortal alike.

"Wait—what?" Val's shocked voice cut in. "He appeared to you *naked*?"

Pip laughed, his lovely head thrown back against the pillow. "What on earth did you think? That he popped right out of the oil lamp in his khakis? Really, Val." Pip's last comment held a scolding humor Jinn surmised he rarely let out, having been so shy about who he was and coy about his desires for so long. This free Pip was a delightful sight.

"Hmm...," Val harrumphed, pouting. His sky-blue eyes raked over Jinn's robust, muscular body, the look so sexy it defied description, and that was definitely a look Jinn relished. "Fair enough," he said, shrugging, but he added a wicked grin. "I wish I'd been there to see it." Giving the guy what he asked for without words, Jinn leaned above Pip just a bit to grab Val by the back of his neck with his own big palm and yank him closer for a delicious kiss.

"Unbelievable...." Pip's amused, slightly reproachful tone huffed beneath them. "You can see him naked in front of you right now!"

Val laughed heartily into the kiss, and his Darjeeling-tea-and-cupcake-scented breath mixed with mint toothpaste and his natural taste, giving Jinn a scrumptious sensory experience, the taste of Val lingering on his tongue and entering as puffs of breath into his lungs. "True." His playful smile made Jinn's heart skip a beat, and his wink made his cock grow harder, hotter, and tighter in a heartbeat. Surprised that Val was the reason for this rapid reaction, Jinn was startled to realize that Val had his heart in his clutches just as much as Pip. "You know, Jinn...," Val said in a hushed tone, smiling affectionately, "even when I was a god I'd heard of your kind. Fiery immortals, slaves to your whims, powers rivaling those of gods."

Jinn grinned. "Apt description, to be sure. And we genies had heard of you, the glacial gods of the far northern expanse, traversing the icy lands beneath the northern lights with your fair Valkyrie companions, enjoying your hearty parties in the grand halls of Valhalla."

"Yes, those were the days…." Val's voice trailed off, and he sighed.

Right then Jinn realized that he and Val had not really spoken to each other much one on one, without Pip's presence, and yet they were a lot alike, as they had more in common with each other than with Pip, a mortal who had not lived long enough to experience the kinds of remarkable things he and Val had. Perhaps the reason for that was the shared knowledge between them that both their pasts held secrets few mortals were privy to, and required even fewer spoken words to be hashed out. One was a genie, the other a god. What they knew and understood about the world could fill planets, suns, and moons—and yet this new mortal existential journey they had both embarked upon held only unknowns. But Jinn and Val were both in love with Pip and would make the same choice every time.

This talk right here, with all three of them bare in flesh and tongue, with Pip beneath them saying nothing and letting them talk uninterrupted, was the closest Jinn and Val had come to a heart to heart, face to face. "Did you regret surrendering your divine powers when you were reborn as a mere mortal?"

Smiling ruefully, Val still shook his head emphatically, and his tender gaze landed on Pip's open, expressive face. "No. Not for a second. No regrets, no doubts, no fears. I'm good." Val looked up at Jinn, the query honest and true in his blue eyes, just ever so slightly worried about the answer. "You?"

At first Jinn couldn't find the strength to speak, but his hesitation dissipated at the warm glow of Val's eyes. "I have many regrets, yes. How could I not since until very recently I was an indentured genie for punishment of my misdeeds, after all." Then his gaze lowered to Pip, and his truth lay there waiting for him to be honest. Jinn had neither the will nor the inclination to deny Pip. "But I have no regrets that involve Pip. None whatsoever."

Pip beamed and blushed at the compliment and rose up on his elbows and craned his neck to catch Jinn's lips, and Jinn gave in to the desire to reciprocate, tilting his head to the side for a better angle to deepen the kiss. A hungry moan from Pip was muffled by the infusion of their lips, and in all his hundreds of years, Jinn had never heard a more delectable sound.

Due to the encompassing nature of the searing kiss, Jinn heard Val's words only faintly, but even then he heard the uncertainty there, the worry, the trepidation. "Does it bother you to share Pip with me?"

Jinn was not the only one gasping into the kiss he broke when Pip's shock was evident in his reactions, mouth gaping and eyes wide open. Jinn turned to face Val, who'd come to lie down at Pip's side, his strong arm brushing Jinn's. "No, Val. For I did not lose half a heart, but I gained two instead. As you gave yours to me, so I give mine to you—both."

The relief in Val came out in a long sigh, as if the man had held his anxious breath for hours. The shaky smile he offered was quickly devoured by Jinn, who took Val's mouth in a smoldering hot, passionate kiss that knew no limits or shame.

The three of them were as one.

And the truth of that was only confirmed when Pip eagerly joined in the kiss, sloppy and chuckling, attempting to entwine and snake his tongue into the mix of entangling tongues. They all began to laugh against each other's lips, too much for the kiss to be anything more than the occasional nibble of teeth, lapping tongues, or brushing lips. Still, for Jinn it was paradise.

This time it was Val who broke from the kiss, leaving Pip and Jinn devouring each other to their hearts' content. Gently he nudged Pip to his side and began to nibble on his shoulders and the nape of his neck. Jinn left the kiss after him, trailing kisses down Pip's cheek and jawline, down to his throat, where he nuzzled and suckled on the bobbing laryngeal prominence, laving it with the flat of his tongue.

"Oh, please," Pip cried out at the sensory attack of two mouths on his skin.

Jinn backed away to grin and to watch Val, whose luscious mouth slid further down Pip's back, licking and sucking and even biting tenderly. Pip whimpered and closed his eyes, clearly enjoying the attention lavished on his supple body with its youthful glow Jinn adored so. Val chuckled against Pip's skin as he drifted down, his lips encircling every bump of Pip's spine, one by one, until he reached the curve of the small of his back and the dip there, kissing it for what seemed like forever.

For Jinn, the view was adorable and arousing, and the love Val poured over Pip was all the message that needed to get across. "You've never been with two men, have you?" Pip's hazel eyes shot open, and he blushed—embarrassed, by the look of things. "That's not a bad thing, sweetheart. You have no idea what it does to me—and I imagine to Val too—to know that we are the first, the last, and the only ones to have you this way."

The shamed coloring evaporated from Pip's cheeks as he gave Jinn a tentative smile. "Really?"

Val must've bitten Pip on the ass cheek then, because Pip jumped and moaned, looking behind him, startled and wide-eyed—until his eyes glazed over and a look of rapture overtook his expressive face. "Absolutely," Val confirmed, touching the curve of Pip's hip and following the trail set by his fingers with his licking tongue. "No one but Jinn and I will ever fuck you like this."

"Oh…," Pip whispered, his face reheating, but this time it was with all-out sexual excitement and lust. "Please, Val, fuck me. Please, Jinn, fuck me now."

Jinn looked at Val, who gave a barely perceptible nod. Quickly, as if they'd done this before, they shifted positions with ease. Jinn lay on his back on the comforter so light a green it was almost white, Pip on top of him only halfway as he lay on his stomach between Jinn's spread legs, and Val sat back on his knees between their legs, his hands wandering all over Pip's lower back and buttocks, squeezing the firm, round white globes with eager delight.

"Eat him up, Val," Jinn encouraged while his own hips bucked ever so slightly at the feel of Pip's silky smooth chest over his groin.

"Don't give him any ideas—*oh!*" Pip cried out when Val used his palms to separate his ass cheeks and moved from the base of Pip's cock to the top of his crease in one smooth lick of his flattened tongue. "Oh my God.…" Jinn chuckled at Pip's response, and those hazel eyes, burning with unbridled dark lust, shot up to meet his. Cocking his head to the side as if to say *"Beware,"* Pip wetted his pink lips, grabbed Jinn's cock in his hand, lowered his head, and swallowed the fat head of Jinn's chocolate-brown cock, running his mouth around the ridge of the crown, tonguing the slit, and sucking the head with furious intent. Jinn shivered. Oh yeah, revenge *was* sweet.

For a while the only sounds heard in the hotel room were wet slurping sounds as Val ate Pip's ass and Pip sucked on Jinn's cock. Val's hums, Pip's whimpers, and Jinn's hisses added to the symphony of sex where every wet lick, brush of skin, and small slap made a unique sound.

Jinn was in the best position possible, with his back against the emerald-green headboard, to watch Pip suck his cock with the same relentless enthusiasm he always exhibited with new projects of interest, and Val eat Pip's ass, his tongue swirling around Pip's puckered pink hole, licking along the crease back and forth, suckling the twitching opening and then jabbing his darted tongue inside the dark heat of Pip's inner channel.

Jinn was well aware what that felt like, both giving and receiving, and Val had an admirable technique of shifting his method of pleasuring and taking his time with everything. As it was, Jinn felt every movement Val made through Pip, whose responses hid nothing. Pip was laid bare and exposed, and he gave all of himself to the two men surrounding him. It was a heady feeling to be trusted so by someone so young and inexperienced, and Jinn wanted to sink his cock into Pip's creamy flesh, to bury himself so deep a part of him would always remain within Pip. But there was another one to be considered first, and that sign of confidence took nothing from Jinn but instead gave him everything.

"Take him, Val. He needs your cock."

Pip moaned against Jinn's dick, the vibrations on his sensitized skin giving him chills. "Yes, please, Val," he affirmed with a raspy whisper that echoed almost like a sob. His hips bucked up and down against the comforter, seeking both the friction of the bed and the pressure of Val's mouth with every frantic motion. His full lips were a darker shade of pink now, wet with saliva and precome, and swollen just enough to create a burst of need within Jinn.

Bracing himself up with one hand, Jinn cupped the back of Pip's neck and brought him forward for a kiss. Pip shivered and moaned so that maintaining the depth and skill of the kiss became impossible, but Jinn gave it all he had—and so did Pip, reaching for him with his sweaty, trembling hands that just made Jinn desire him more. Of all the lovers of his past in the seraglio and the vast cities of the jinn, Pip was by far the shyest, the sweetest, and the most innocent. Jinn had no desire to tarnish or corrupt him, to dirty him up, or to whisk him off to decadence. He loved Pip as he was now.

"Oh God," Pip blurted out in a huff of hot air when, behind him, Val's cock breached the snug ring of muscle. Jinn allowed the young man to lower and rest his face against Jinn's taut, ripped abdomen, groaning and shuddering with pleasure, and jolting when Val found his rhythm, keeping a steady slow pace with the occasional faster, harder, and deeper thrust. Jinn saw Val's bright red cock surging into Pip's pale body, and it was the most erotic sight he'd ever witnessed. And inside his heart he knew the reason for that was the emotional bond they shared.

Their love intensified their sex.

Pip's raised bottom dropped when his knees gave out, and he fell flat on his stomach on the mattress between Jinn's open legs. Straightening, Pip half sobbed, half moaned against Jinn's bronze-hued skin, grabbing his flanks, his fingers digging in painfully for leverage and comfort. Jinn caressed Pip's sandy-brown hair, tenderly tugging on the strands, and gave him all the reassurance he needed in the arms of two men.

"Oh, so big," Pip mumbled incoherently, his hips trying to raise up again, but Val's body came down on top of him, Val's abdomen against the small of Pip's back, as Val kept himself up with his straightened arms between Pip's torso and Jinn's thighs. The light coating of honey-golden fuzz on Val's lean yet muscular chest must've tickled Pip's smooth, sweaty back, Jinn was certain of it, and grinned. Val quickened the pace of his fucking, a look of sheer bliss plastered all over his heated red face dotted by a swarm of golden freckles—and only Jinn was privy to that view as Pip buried his face against Jinn's ripped stomach.

Jinn didn't care that his cock was painfully hard and sandwiched without means of release between his own belly and Pip's chest. It felt too good to feel every push Val made as a jolt on Pip's body, and Pip's smooth, lanky chest rubbed Jinn's cock back and forth in delicious friction.

Suddenly Val leaned down over Pip's shoulder and with his mouth reached down to scoop Jinn's cock into his wet heat, licking and sucking on the head with such fierceness Jinn nearly blew right then and there. He hissed at the pressure of it, loving the feel of an unfamiliar mouth taking him to the edge of delight, especially since the man doing it was no stranger.

"Yes, give it to me, Váli," he urged in a hoarse whisper.

And then his imagination exploded into fireworks when Pip lifted ever so gently and turned his head, licking Jinn's erect member again, up and down the length of the uncut cock, smothering it with openmouthed, suckling kisses. And all the while, the apparently quite mystifyingly acrobatic Val was not only sucking on the head of Jinn's dick over Pip's shoulder but pounding into Pip's ass with ferocity.

Whatever apprehension Jinn had felt about being on the sidelines of Pip and Val's first lovemaking session evaporated with the heat rising from his insides through the pores of his skin. He wasn't the third wheel. He was the cherished, wanted, and needed equal in a threesome. Theirs was a love triangle, not one of jealousy and adultery, but one where all partners belonged to each other and with one another. Love was an adventure, and their threesome was triply so.

"I love you," Pip murmured in between them, Val's cock in his ass and Jinn's dick in his mouth. And Jinn knew he directed his words to both of them—and to all of them in unison. Jinn couldn't wait to take Val's place behind that perfect bubble-butt of Pip's and shove his big fat cock inside that tight dark heat with all the hunger he felt within.

And there was still Val's suggestion to enact. Val caught in between Jinn and Pip, Jinn inside Val and Val inside Pip. Breathless with want over the delicious scenarios playing in his mind, he could barely sit still and let these two men pleasure his cock. The images in his head and in front of him were both provocative enough that the physical response was mere icing on the cake. Jinn had amorous feelings for Pip, and Val was absolutely beginning to grow on him.

Feelings and sensations mixed, and Jinn's heart knew no way to separate them anymore.

This time Jinn was playing for keeps.

As Jinn leaned forward, his abdominal muscles straining, Pip let go of Jinn's cock with a wet pop, cupped Jinn's cheek with hot and shaky hands, and drew him into a kiss so breathless and out of control with moaning and panting that it lacked style and depth, but it was heavy and succulent with intensity and hunger.

"You're so hot and so kissable," Pip mumbled into the kiss, and Jinn chuckled. The reward for that was a sharp nibble on his lower lip where Pip bit down in punishment, giving Jinn shivers.

Trapped in an awkward half-sitting position and lost briefly in Pip's kiss, Jinn faintly registered Val letting go of his cock. Pip's cry against Jinn's lips as he broke the kiss told Jinn about Val's actions, and as he opened his eyes, he did indeed see Val's teeth latch onto Pip's shoulder. More than a soft nip but less than a fierce love bite, seeing it made Jinn's heart flutter.

But he wanted to play too, so he grabbed Pip's arms and dragged the young man higher on top of him until their faces were almost level and he could thrust his tongue down Pip's throat more forcefully and deeper, probing and savoring.

"I'll get you for that, Jinn," Val growled behind Pip, having popped out of Pip in the process of Jinn pulling Pip into his arms. Jinn chuckled into the kiss. Yes, he had no doubt there'd be retribution, but it would be delicious.

And when Val joined in on the three-way kiss, Jinn's salacious sanctions turned sacred and sensuous. The stimulation of the tongues and lips and teeth of two men was an experience Jinn had felt before—but not with two men he cared for to this extent. As it was, there was enjoyment and frustration combined as their lust pushed them forward to seek each other out, but the inability of three sets of lips to lock together was nerve-wracking. And yet, this mix of emotions served to enhance the pleasure of the carnal and erotic moment. And after a while, it no longer mattered whose mouth was where, as all their lips felt and tasted the same as they shared breath, saliva, and touch.

Val's lips drifted down over Jinn's throat, and the nip he gave him made Jinn shudder. His desire for the unbridled, unhindered sexual power of Val kindled his fire within, and as a result Jinn no longer knew which one, Pip or Val, he wanted to fuck first.

Val decided for him, moving back and staring down at Jinn with eyes hooded with lust so their sky-like blueness resembled a night sky. "Fuck me now, Jinn." His voice quivered, undecided whether it meant to be commanding or pleading.

But that did not matter to Jinn, who quickly gave a light nod, and when Val backed off, Jinn tipped Pip off his chest, turning him flat on his back. Quickly and expertly, with instinctive unity, Jinn and Val repositioned themselves around and over Pip, who lay on the plump mattress, silently waiting for whatever was to come. This sweet act of trust, loyalty, and devotion gave Jinn heart palpitations.

Pip, though, was about to show how little good it did to try and anticipate his actions. Val kneeled on the bed between Pip's legs, and Jinn repositioned himself behind Val's strong back, pushing the man to bend forward and raise his ass for Jinn's gently probing fingers. As Jinn parted those firm, athletic buttocks and dipped his head to give the small of Val's back a tiny tentative lick, Val groaned and dropped down further, almost falling over Pip.

Suddenly Pip scrambled up on his knees and held Val up, grinning as he traced Val's lips with his own. All this Jinn felt through the skin of his palms caressing Val's taut, trembling butt and saw as he lifted his head to peer at what was happening when he felt the bed sway as Pip moved around. What Jinn didn't expect was Pip's words.

"Oh God, Val. You look so hot with Jinn's tongue in your ass. Let him lick you, let him suck you, let him fuck you. I want to see you weak with need. I want to see your face when he rams that gargantuan cock inside you. I want to kiss you breathless when you engulf all of Jinn's cock with your ass."

Both Jinn and Val gawked at Pip with their mouths hanging open in surprise. The soft sound emerged from Val's throat, a sigh wrapped up in a gurgle, and Jinn did not need to see Val's expression to feel the same shock, bewilderment, and amusement that the former Norse god felt. Pip blushed all over his face, neck, and chest, but despite the nervousness consuming him, he didn't back away or stop the eye contact with Val.

Swallowing hard, Val spoke in a hoarse voice so deep with raw lust that Jinn almost didn't recognize it. "Jinn? Do all those things to me. Now, please."

Smiling, Jinn did not need to be told twice. Pip gave him a glance filled with love and joy and passion, and that one gesture fueled Jinn's desire. With a voracious appetite, Jinn lowered onto the bed, pushing Val down with his palm on the small of his back, feeling the muscles and tendons there jumping and shivering under his touch. Val practically keeled over, a giggling Pip gathered the man up in his embrace, and Jinn chuckled against Val's most intimate nether regions.

"Hey, not so rough," Val admonished, teetering above Pip, but Jinn could hear he wasn't serious. It seemed the Norse god who was now a mortal man liked being manhandled.

Parting those luscious lumps of flesh again, Jinn licked his way down the perineum to softly suckle on Val's scrotum, lapping the tender sac all over before retreating back up to lick his anus, first around the pucker, swirling the twitching rim round and round, and then flicking the tip of his tongue into the hole. He opened his mouth wider to surround the orifice with his lips, kissing and suckling in between sharp jabs of his tongue.

Val moaned, but the noise was muffled, so Jinn knew Pip was kissing the man breathless just like he'd promised. Jinn wondered what Val must've felt at that moment, having a tongue piercing and exploring not one but two of his bodily cavities simultaneously. In fact, Jinn did know, as he too had been in this position before. But there had not been a love component to the process then, so Jinn doubted it would've felt the same.

Val's next words confirmed as much as he huffed into Pip's kiss, "Oh, Jinn, you have got to feel this."

Laughing against the wet, sensitive skin so that Val shuddered, Jinn said, "All in good time, dear boy. Now, spread those legs for me so I can lavish you with my tongue."

Devoting all his immense attention and considerable skill to tongue-bathing Val, Jinn relished the masculine musky scent of Val's rear end, the smooth skin of his crease with its light coating of golden fuzz, the soft warmth of his balls, and the tight, hot heaviness of his cock as Jinn reached for Val's cock, that was near bursting. Working the cock gently with the dry heat of his hand, Jinn licked the inside of his palm and continued stroking Val's cock, thumbing the slit at the top, gathering up the milky droplets of precome and spreading them all over the uncut cock burning all fiery red. And all the while his tongue did wicked, naughty things to Val's asshole.

"Oh, damn, Jinn," Val whispered wantonly. "You're driving me crazy."

Pip chuckled, apparently kissing Val's face now instead of his lips since the sound his smacks made changed slightly. "You look great all crazed and dazed, babe." The hesitant term of endearment caused Val to gasp and, from the sound of it, draw the young man into a fervent kiss. So, it was an experiment with successful results. Jinn smiled.

Stopping, Jinn got up to sit on his heels, licking the taste of Val off his lips. "All right, dear boys. Time to get these proceedings trotting along, don't you think?" Wrapping his right arm around Val's trim waist, Jinn yanked the man up on his heels and pressed Val flush against his own body, his hot, hard cock lodged between Val's ass cheeks, rubbing along the crevice up and down. "Do you like that, sweetheart?"

Val's blond head dropped back over Jinn's shoulder as he sighed and muttered, "Oh, by the gods, yes, Jinn. So good." Val's smooth, athletic form, leaner than Jinn himself, made Jinn's belly lurch and his heart flip as the man's ripped muscles flexed and rippled underneath his touch. With passion coursing through his veins, Jinn ran his hands all over Val's taut body, caressing silken planes, gripping hard curves, and squeezing the red disks of his nipples until they pebbled into jutting nubs. Val groaned in desperation as his hips snapped forward and rocked back, his back arching. "Oh, damn, no more," he growled, pushing himself out of Jinn's embrace, turning around, fumbling, cupping Jinn's face and pulling him into a feverishly hot kiss, more heaving breaths than tongues playing, more blind groping than intimate smooching. Val had never been this domineering, even with Pip, and Jinn was secretly over the moon that Val had chosen him for this.

"Oh my God...," Pip's small voice whispered nearby. "I want you both to fuck me out of this world."

Jinn broke the kiss, absently noting the dazed and sex-tousled look Val was sporting already, and turned to Pip, who bit his lower lip anxiously. He seemed to want to verbalize his sexual desires and give voice to his need for the two men, but he was unsure of the reception of such a speech. Jinn set out to reassure him in the best way he knew how.

"On your back, dear boy. Knees up. Raise that pretty little bottom of yours so Val can shove that beautiful cock into your ass balls-deep and fuck you till you scream. And when he's done I'm going to flip you over on your stomach, push my big cock inside you, and fuck you so hard you will forget your name and where you are. And then, when you're all loose and relaxed, sweaty and hot, both Val and I are going back in for round two. He'll ream your ass while my cock plays with that pretty little mouth of yours. And we'll do it for hours on end."

Pip's hazel eyes widened as big as saucers, and then they darkened to a hue of chocolate brown as he more involuntarily swooned than purposely fell flat on his back in front of the two men. Gasping and panting, he whispered only one word in a shaky voice: "Please."

Watching Pip's movements and listening to his plea, Val glanced over his shoulder at Jinn, who nodded. His attention back on track, Val slid his fingers lightly over Pip's thighs as Pip held his legs up against his chest with his hands behind his bent knees. "I love the way your skin feels. So soft. So silky smooth," Val said with admiration. Peering over Val's shoulder, Jinn watched Val's hands shift and his eyes move to lock with Pip's. "You're so beautiful. I've coveted you for so long, love, that I just want to devour every inch of you."

"That makes two of us," Jinn whispered in Val's ear, and Val turned his profile to him, craning his neck to steal a kiss from the genie's lips. "You give our dear boy's derriere the attention it deserves while I get the lube." Scurrying off the bed, Jinn went straight for the nightstand, where Val had stored the lubricant they had yet to try out in practice. This one was mint-scented and apparently created a tingling sensation when applied on the lower erogenous zones. Jinn couldn't wait to try out this new substance, as he was more familiar with the body oils with fragrances of lavender, vanilla, and roses that genies used.

Back on the bed, Jinn observed in amusement the heavy-duty frotting going on as Val lay on top of Pip, their bodies and especially their cocks grinding against each other in delicious friction eased by the precome oozing out of the slits of their cocks.

For a moment Jinn was content only to watch, as the sight filled him with not just lust but with love. He hadn't known these two men for long, but in that short time he'd learned their deepest, darkest secrets and their inner selves, had come to know their personalities in words and deeds, and felt an instinctive connection with them as strongly as they did with him.

Jinn had often wondered if it was indeed possible to fall in love so easily and so quickly, to get to know someone—let alone two people—in what amounted to a blink of an eye, and to start building a relationship on a foundation that had not yet stood the test of time, though the three of them had lived to tell the tale of deadly enemies, traps in an underground maze, and the truths held within their hearts.

The lovemaking of Val and Pip was a beautiful sight, and Jinn couldn't get enough of that privileged view until....

Val parted from Pip's lips and turned to Jinn with an honest query in his now midnight-blue eyes. "You coming, Jinn? It's not just my ass that needs you over here." Jinn chuckled warmly. It wasn't the most subtle or romantic come-hither he'd ever heard, but it was the most heartfelt.

Climbing on the bed again, Jinn dropped the lube on the coverlet next to them and repositioned himself behind Val, grabbing and pulling his hips up and off Pip, rubbing his smoldering hot and hard-as-steel erection between Val's butt cheeks.

"Oh, yeah, just like that, right there," Val moaned. "Give it to me, Jinn. I need you."

Jinn laughed teasingly. "Thank you, sweetheart, but I don't need a tour guide for this."

Giggling, Pip winked at him and said, "Oh, Jinn. You *do* give it to him good."

Val gave them both a scowl.

Pip's slender hands still kept moving up and down Val's arms, which were braced against the mattress, so Jinn resumed eating Val's ass with a vengeance, suckling on the soft spot just below Val's pucker, toward his balls. It didn't take long for him to hear not just Val moaning but the plastic top of the lube tube popping open, and the sound of the mint-scented jelly squirted over fingers. Val's position shifted when he held himself up with only his left hand as his right toyed with Pip's puckered hole, pink and beckoning, with his lubed-up fingers. The whimpering from Pip rang familiar in Jinn's ears, having heard it before, but now he found he longed to keep hearing it.

Running his palms over the backs of Val's thighs and down between his legs to caress the silkier, more tender inner thighs, Jinn licked a long unbroken line down to Val's balls and then back up along the soft crease past the opening to the dip in the small of his back, kissing the sweaty skin there. Groaning, Val rocked back toward him, and Jinn coveted more contact with the Norse god's skin, lapping all over Val's back with the flat of his tongue. Upon reaching his shoulder, Jinn bit down at the soft junction of neck and shoulder, then smoothed the sting away with his tongue. Val turned his head, and they kissed. His light-golden stubble rasped against Jinn's smooth skin.

"I love watching you two kiss. It's the most erotic thing I've ever seen." Pip's mesmerized voice was filled with awe and adoration.

Val grinned lewdly into his kiss with Jinn. "When I saw you and Jinn kiss back at the tent, I wanted to kill Jinn." In the background, Pip gasped in shock. Drawing back, Jinn studied Val's face, a whole host of emotions—from frustration and jealousy to shame and regret—present and battling for dominance. But then caring and the warmth of love replaced them, and Val smiled ruefully. "But I know now the kind of man you are, Jinn. And I would wish no one else for Pip—or for me. We are blessed to have you in our lives. And though I may not have initially been the sort of man you'd want to be around, let alone be with, I hope you know that so much, everything, really, has changed since then. I love Pip—and I love you. It's true I don't know all about you yet, nor you about me, but we'll get there, won't we?"

Jinn wound his right hand around Val's chest, and he threaded his left through Val's golden blond hair, smiling affectionately. "Yes, sweetheart. We will. I imagine it will be some time before we get to go back to Majlis al Jinn. I do believe you said you have a place in this country?"

"Val doesn't have a place here," Pip chuckled. "He has an *estate*."

Giving a chiding look at Pip, Val looked sheepish when his eyes returned to Jinn. "Yes, I do suppose that description is as apt as any. My mortal lineage is both Viking and Norman. I have an ancestral estate—a very small settlement with a tiny manor-type of cottage—in the south of England."

"Small settlement? Tiny manor?" Pip's feigned chagrined look caused Val's cheeks to redden at the taunting. Jinn smiled, liking the way the two men interacted, indicating with ease all the familiarity they felt for each other. He felt privileged to be a part of them in this threesome of love, devotion, and sex. Pip spoke to Jinn with clear enunciation, obviously for the benefit of scolding Val. "The settlement is composed of three villages, and the manor has near a hundred rooms—"

"There are barely a hundred people altogether living in those rundown hamlets," Val interjected with righteous indignation. "And Pip is exaggerating as there are maybe a dozen or two rooms, most of them unlivable." Pip sneered at the explanation but thankfully said nothing, and Val sighed. "Can we now get on with this, Pip my love? Or do you maybe want to hash out my Norman lineage down to the first ancestor since the days of William the Conqueror? Or perhaps you want to explore even further back in time to the first Vikings back in medieval times?"

At first Pip had been merely giggling. Now he was chortling. "Oh, Val, you're so sexy when you get all flustered and frustrated and—"

"I'll show you flustered," Val growled. He scooped up Pip's buttocks, yanked him into his lap in a rash motion, and pressed the blunt red tip of his cock past the tight ring of muscle inside Pip's hot, dark channel. A thrill shot through Pip, who hissed like a snake, then moaned loudly, and whose hips shot up fast and frantic, but Val's firm grip held. In fact, Val pushed Pip's knees more forcefully against his chest by the backs of his thighs, pulling back until only the tip of his cock remained seated within Pip and then thrusting back in slowly but deep.

"Oh my God, so deep, so big," Pip mumbled. Then he cried out as Val pulled out again and then pushed back in.

Pip whimpered as Val set his pace, all the while staring down at him. "Still feel like teasing, love?" Jinn suppressed a laugh as Pip's fluttering eyes shot open and gave a pointed, fierce look back, almost growling, but since he was so enraptured with pleasure it came out a sweet purr.

"Jinn?" Pip said instead, still maintaining eye contact with Val, and Jinn knew beforehand what Pip was about to say. "Shut that blustering ox up with your cock. Ram into him like there's no tomorrow."

"As you wish, sweetheart." Jinn kissed the nape of Val's neck tenderly, comfortingly. "Are you ready, dear boy?"

Val nodded eagerly, glancing back at him. "Fuck me, Jinn. Fuck Pip through me. Fuck us both into ecstasy."

"As you wish." Both Val and Pip gave a short chuckle at that, and they both looked at Jinn with such sweet love that Jinn felt like he might explode with the fire of it burning in his heart.

Grabbing the tube of lube, Jinn popped the barely closed lip open, smeared his fingers with the cool mint-scented jelly, and began testing the rim of Val's quivering opening. But Val's thrusting movements made it impossible to continue the sensual torment, especially since that eager ass attempted time and again to swallow the questing finger. Jinn's own cock stood so hard, hot, and heavy that he didn't dare to prolong the experience beyond either of their tolerances. Shoving a probing finger inside Val's narrow heat up to the first knuckle, Jinn felt Val's inner muscles clamp down on him and then let go, sucking his exploring digit in further. The scent of male musk grew stronger, and Jinn inhaled deeply.

"Oh, Jinn," Val huffed, straining between Pip and Jinn, barely moving inside Pip at all, waiting for the genie's entry. "I need your cock, dammit." Chuckling, Jinn found Val's lack of control and his use of profanities most charming.

In short order, Jinn gave Val's tight passage a second and then a third finger, pushing in all the way, until his twisting fingers learned all they needed to for maximum pleasure. Val shook and groaned when Jinn's fingers jabbed at his sweet spot. "Like this, Váli? Love what I'm doing to you? Want me to fuck you?"

"Yes, dammit," Val growled breathlessly, his muscles trembling and his skin sweating. "Fuck me already, Jinn, or I swear I will—"

"I do believe you're swearing enough for all of us, sweetheart," Jinn taunted.

Hearing Val draw breath to start either snarling or cursing, Jinn pulled out his fingers, used the remaining jelly on his fingers to slick and coat his dark-brown cock, aligned himself swiftly, and then pushed past the snug ring of muscles in one sharp lunge forward.

"Oh, fuck," Val cursed, his head thrown back against Jinn's shoulder, almost smacking him right on the nose. Jinn gripped his hips, which shivered uncontrollably, trying to push forward and back at once, to escape from the invasion into Pip's tight heat and to reach back for Jinn's hard cock sinking deeper into him. "Oh, fuck, yeah, right there."

Apparently in one fell swoop Jinn had managed to ram his cock against Val's sweet spot, so digging his fingers in deeper, Jinn pulled out and pushed back in fast, hard, and deep. Val moaned— and then Pip whimpered, indicating Val's cock had slid deeper into Pip too.

"Do I please you both, sweethearts?"

"Oh, Jinn," Pip murmured, his hands squeezing Val's straight arms. "More, Val. More, Jinn. I need."

"Yeah, Jinn," Val huffed, as if in agony, but that sweet delight was all pleasure as he swayed and swiveled his hips to get more room as Jinn kept thrusting his cock in and out in a primitive rhythm. "I need your cock." Clearly, being sandwiched between his two lovers was a position Val loved with every feverish breath, and Jinn grinned, rocking his hips to the sides and then back and forth, slowing his pace to deep, forceful thrusts that would pass through Val all the way to Pip. And from the simultaneous moaning from his lovers, Jinn knew he'd succeeded.

"One day I will make love to you both under the bright sun under palm trees in an oasis, and one night I will love you both under the pale moonlight in a bed big enough for the three of us." Jinn spoke the words from his heart.

"Oh, yes, please, take us there," Pip whispered, whimpering as each and every one of Jinn's rocking motions echoed through Val into him. Jinn kept slamming into Val's tight, hot channel that welcomed him with its massaging muscles, and the closeness he felt to both men suffused his very being, as if their love was tangible fiery liquid seeping into his body, heart, and soul through osmosis. The feeling only intensified as the jelly heated and tingled all over his cock, and he wondered how it felt in both Val's and Pip's tight channels.

Val lifted his left arm and wound it shakily around Jinn's neck as he tilted his head for a kiss. That panting mouth with its pliant lips gave Jinn every reassurance of love he could hope for. Tasting that sweet, tea-scented breath, so like Pip's, only a little less sweet and muskier, Jinn curled and entwined his tongue with Val's. The man's grip on his neck and long hair increased with every passionate inhale.

"I want those things, Jinn," Val finally managed to mumble against his lips, panting wildly. "I want to see you dancing on golden sands and skinny-dipping in a cool pool surrounded by a lush green oasis. I want you and Pip with me all the time. I want us to travel the world and see its many wonders and fall in love with each other deeper than ever before."

Jinn smiled. "And we shall have all those things. I promise."

Val nudged Jinn's cheek with his nose in an Eskimo kiss. "I can't wait."

"You want to stop so we can do those things now?" Jinn teased, grinning.

Val's blue eyes flashed and then darkened as he growled, "Don't you dare."

Resolutely, Jinn removed Val's arm from around his neck and gently placed Val's palm on Pip's inner thigh again, pushing Val forward by the weight of his torso as he interlaced their fingers. And all the while Jinn kept a constant, steady stream of shallow short thrusts into Val, pushing the man into Pip over and over again.

Val chuckled breathlessly. "Your hair is tickling me."

Swinging his head and flipping his long black hair all around, like a lion shaking his mane, Jinn laughed, the sound reverberating onto his cock and from there to both Val and Pip. His long hair did flow down in feather-like cascades of black strands brushing over Val's smooth, muscular back, slick with sweat, and reaching even Pip's chest and face over Val's sides.

Pip giggled happily and with his hands caught a few strands, winding them around his fingers and giving them gentle tugs. "I love your hair, Jinn. Promise me you will never cut it."

Jinn looked over Val's shoulder at his sweetest wish master and his lover, giving his second promise of the night and meaning it from the depth of his soul. "I promise."

The blissful expression Pip demonstrated along with his open smile, graced by dimples, was all Jinn needed. And when smiling Val glanced back at him, his cloud of golden freckles clearly visible on his flushed face, Jinn knew he also had everything he'd wanted for as long as he could remember. In all his years, like a bee rushing from one blossom to the next seeking nectar, Jinn had explored a vast, complex array of sexual partners—but though they spoke of love and acted scenes of love, he'd never been in love.

Now he was, and it was more than he ever could've imagined.

"Val, take Pip in hand. I'll ride you both."

The hoarse, sexy command from Jinn was met with eager willingness to obey, and Val moved his right hand to fulfill the order by fisting the base of Pip's pink cock, lying heavy and hot on his belly, dripping precome. Jinn grabbed Val's hips again in a firm hold and began to pound him into orbit and beyond. Val shuddered and groaned, almost falling flat over Pip, whose delicate frame might not have withstood that. But Val's left arm supported his weight, and Jinn's fiery grip did the rest.

In unison, they found their rhythm in motions, actions, and reactions, when Jinn pushed in, forcing Val forward deeper into Pip, lying on the bed on his back, arching his back and thrashing his head about on the plump pillow, his face sliding effortlessly over the silky pillow case. The combined cadence of their sex-induced inarticulate noises—Jinn's grunts, Val's groans, and Pip's whimpers—added to the age-old beat of their bodies working together toward inevitable climax. At first the sounds came right after each other, as reactions from one to the other and to the third, but soon they overlapped in a unified song of sex.

A sheen of sweat covered Jinn's entire body, he trembled, and his hold on Val began to waver as his need to come overcame his rational side and his instincts took over. No longer in control of his movements, his hips surged of their own volition, jerky and erratic, seeking more friction, more pressure, more contact, and final release.

"I love your pretty dick, love," Val complimented Pip with his raspy tone as his hand glided and stroked the long pink prick with fervor and serious intent, flicking his thumb on the slit every time he reached the top. "And I love your huge cock, Jinn. I want you in me, to fill me to the brim. Fuck me harder, Jinn. I need more."

"Happy to oblige," Jinn whispered in his ear, increasing the pace of his thrusts as he plowed into Val's ass, those firm toned globes bouncing and hitting against his groin until the slapping sounds of their groins, thighs, and bellies grew stronger with every touch, filling the air. When Val moaned loudly, wantonly, and his whole body quaked, Jinn knew he'd once more hit the sweet spot within the man. Chuckling low, as he, too, was beginning to feel the strain of their prolonged lovemaking, Jinn fucked Val with all his might, no longer taking it soft and easy.

"Oh, fuck, yeah," Val moaned. "Just like that. Right there. Oh, fuck." Apparently Val liked his ride rough, Jinn concluded, and gave his lover what he asked for. This method induced a litany of foul language as well, and Jinn found that not only curious but sort of endearing. The sophisticated scholar lost his charming control.

As if reading Jinn's mind, Pip chuckled, out of breath too. "Oh, Val, love the way you talk trash when Jinn is giving it to you good." Hazel eyes wide, Pip watched Jinn over Val's shoulder and smiled. Pip's cheeks, neck, and chest were stained red with arousal, and his hands had lowered to fist the sheets. He looked positively yummy to Jinn, who grinned back and winked.

"What are you two up to?" Val whispered, too caught up in his excitement to muster any actual speaking voice. His gaze darted back and forth, and Jinn stopped him by mashing his mouth over Val's in a conquering, demanding kiss. In the background, Pip's moans grew louder with every brush of teasing tongue the young man could discern, so Jinn knew it was time.

"Pump Pip harder," Jinn ordered Val, breaking the kiss and biting him on the shoulder.

Groaning in part pain, part pleasure, Val dedicated his renewed efforts to bringing Pip to climax, speeding up his fierce stroking of Pip's prick and his own thrusts into Pip's ass. Jinn followed suit, pushing Val forward even more for leverage to buck inside Val's ass harder and deeper. Those inner muscles clamped down on him, milking his cock, and with a thundering roar Val came, shooting his load into Pip, whose slender body jerked and convulsed as he felt Val's climax within his passage. Ropes of snow-white come erupted from Pip's pulsating cock so profoundly that some landed as high as his neck and chin.

"Jinn, please," Val panted, his hips shuddering with the strain when his release had made his tight channel even more sensitized to penetration.

That weak plea, uttered in the vulnerable frenzy of the peak of pleasure exceeded, was all Jinn needed as his sexual need went into overdrive. Liquid fire in the form of a fountain of come exploded out of his cock and spurted into Val's ass, perfusing throughout, until Val was left gasping. With what remained of his inner strength, Jinn pushed into Val still, his cock sliding on the warm bath of his own come easily and effortlessly. He could not stop the smooth glide of his cock as his hips continued their involuntary, instinctive thrill, demanding more of those rhythmic contractions dancing and vibrating along the length of his shaft buried deep within a man he'd come to respect and adore.

"Oh my God…," Pip muttered, puffing out hot gusts of air.

"Fuck yeah," Val agreed. His shaky arms lost their strength, and Val slumped on top of Pip, who oomphed at the weight on him. "Sorry, love," he whispered, trying to gain power within himself to get up and move over.

Keeping his hold on Val's trembling hips, Jinn lifted the man off Pip—and himself out of Val's ass—and laid him down on the bed next to Pip, who smiled back feebly, sated.

Basking in the afterglow of the best sex of his life, Jinn sat back on his heels, allowing himself time to regain his sense of self and his composure. He wasn't prepared to dismiss the slow burn under his skin just yet, as the tingling aftereffect of the sexual high still roamed within and wracked his body, and he closed his eyes to better relish the sensation.

Val's soft, concerned voice awoke him from his reverie. "Pip, what's wrong? Are you hurt? Did we—"

Jinn opened his eyes, startled, and found Pip lying next to Val, his shoulders shimmying with silent sobs, but Pip shook his head emphatically. "No. You were perfect, Val. You too, Jinn. It was perfect. I love you both so much. I never want us to be apart."

"Then what?" Val said, his hands shaking as they sought to touch and comfort Pip. "Love, you're scaring me."

Pip opened his eyes, his long dark lashes like curtains with pearl-like tears attached to them. Quickly he leaned toward Val and kissed him softly, barely skimming the tip of his tongue across Val's lips. "It's just I've never…. This was so intense, and I…." Turning to Jinn, Pip extended his hand invitingly, and Jinn clasped his hand with his own, allowing Pip to pull him down to lie next to him. "My beautiful genie," he whispered, love and awe evident in his tender voice, and he kissed Jinn, all but smothering him with the gentleness of it. In response, Jinn scooped some of Pip's creamy essence from his belly and broke the kiss to bring his fingers to his mouth, licking his hand clean, reveling in the zest of his lover. "Oh," was the only sound Pip seemed capable of producing.

"That's damn hot," Val said to Jinn from Pip's other side, scooting up closer until they had Pip sandwiched between their bigger muscular bodies, still hot and hard from their previous sexual exertions. Val glided his fingers through the whitish blotches of come, and then he too brought the taste to his lips, sucking his fingers, savoring the taste with an exalted look on his face.

"Oh my God...," Pip murmured as he watched Val's movements without blinking.

Suddenly Val grinned, all feral. "I kind of like the idea of you worshiping me as your god of love and sex."

Jinn laughed as Pip stared for a second at Val, dumbfounded and blushing. "Any specific acts of devotion you'd prefer, oh god of gods? Perhaps prostrations on our hands and knees? Holy communion through lovemaking? Blessed come to drink? Sacred cock to eat?"

"Shameless blasphemer." Val chuckled, shaking his head in disbelief. "I was never a god people worshiped daily or said prayers to. And," he added, glancing at Pip, "my lovers need not resort to prayer to get my attention." Giving Jinn a playfully scolding stare, he said, "And besides, you're one to talk. Yes, you may not require prayers but wishes to fulfill, but as mortals are belief bearers of the gods, so are mortals wish masters to you. Our situations and positions are not that dissimilar."

Jinn acquiesced with an honoring bow of his head. "As you wish, sweetheart. What I wish to know is, will you smite me down if I do not please you, oh deity of delight?"

Val laughed in earnest, his blond head thrown back. "And what will you do with your newfound freedom, oh genie of jest? Snap your fingers and magically turn this room into a harem of willing love slaves? Or perhaps a steamy Turkish bath where the nudity before you is mandatory?"

Jinn shook his head, not breaking eye contact while teasing Val. "No, dear boy. What use would I have for love slaves when I have the two of you? As enticing as a bath or a seraglio does sound, I have something else in mind. And hopefully I won't need to snap my fingers to make it all happen."

"What, then?" Pip inquired, and both men turned their gazes down to see the lovely young man between them.

"I've told you," Jinn reminded them both, "as soon as you've regained your strength, Pip, I'm going to flip you over and shove my big cock inside you. While I do that, Val will put his huge cock in your mouth. And then we will fuck you, sweetheart, until you scream."

Pip's face flushed—and his spent dick jumped on his stomach.

Val's fingers caressed the half-hard cock back to life with a dreamy expression on his face. "And, just like Jinn promised, after that we will take a wee catnap—and move on to round three." Looking up at Jinn through his golden lashes, he asked wickedly, "What shall we do with Pip then? Because I was thinking we'd take Pip out to my place tomorrow in Cornwall, and there we'd both fuck that sweet ass of his—at the same time."

Pip's hushed gasp was filled with shock. Then the sound turned into a moan as the image sank in. "Oh, Val, yes, I want that." His darkened gaze darted to Jinn, his hazel eyes burning with desire again, his pupils dilated with lust. "I want that, Jinn. With you two. No one else."

"Only you, sweetheart," Jinn confirmed with a smile, kissing Pip on the lips, brushing his tongue over the seam of his lips, parting them and snaking in, mixing the taste of Pip's come with the flavor of his mouth, and it was divinely delectable.

"Yes, only you two," Val agreed, his hot breath fanning over their faces as he hovered close, nearing their kiss with his lips, joining in on the kiss until their tongues entwined and curled around each other hungrily.

Jinn broke the kiss first, grinning lasciviously. "And now... second movement before crescendo." His imagination provided a libidinous cavalcade of sultry images, tastes, and sounds all rolled up into one as he prepared himself inwardly for more lovemaking with his two sexy lovers. They looked up at him, waiting and wanting, handing him the reins.

Looking at Pip and Val lying on the bed side by side, hugging each other and him, Jinn felt wanted and needed. He felt special. He felt loved. Like he'd found his purpose in the loving threesome with these two beautiful men. Like he'd walked through a personal purgatory of punishment, but it was now all over and done with. Like he'd at long last come home.

And that was his wish come true.

SUSAN LAINE was born and raised in Finland to the best mother in the world, and she told her daughter time and again that she could be and do whatever she wanted in her life. However, it took her until her thirties to find the spark for serious writing by discovering the gay erotic romance genre which is what she mainly writes today.

Her formal education revolves around anthropology, but wishing in time to become a full-time writer Susan does office work at her unfortunately necessary evil day job. When not working or writing (yes, it's her second job), Susan enjoys hanging out with her sister and friends in movie theaters and bookstores. Her other pastimes include walking, swimming, and fantasizing about sizzling hot manlove. Some of her likes are Lady Gaga, chocolate, and doing the dishes (it's relaxing), and a few dislikes are sweating hot summer days, tobacco smoke, and purposeful prejudice. She hopes to one day write a historical romance novel and a murder mystery, too, but all in good time—and there will undoubtedly be a gay romantic twist.

Visit Susan's website at http://www.susan-laine-author.fi/ or write her an e-mail at susan.laine@hotmail.com.

Also from SUSAN LAINE

Sounds of Love

Susan Laine

Romance from SUSAN LAINE